"It's A I

And apparently the c
were laid out for him ᴏ... ...ᴘᴛᴏᴘ.

Even when she got all prim and proper on him, Aidan wanted her.

And now that he'd given himself permission to want her, he couldn't seem to stop. If listening to her presentation meant having her in his bed, he would get through this.

But as she went through her slides, he had to interrupt. "Only at night? What about mornings? Or lunchtime? We could use my conference table… The thing is, I don't think we should be too rigid about this. In fact…"

He slipped his arm around her and walked her to the couch. "I think it'll take a lot of pressue off you if we start practicing right away."

Dear Reader,

I'm a sucker for a good old-fashioned office romance.
Isn't everyone? I think it's because the boss-employee
relationship is considered so taboo these days and it's
a real challenge to turn "forbidden love" into "happily
ever after." But since I love a good challenge as much as
anyone, let me introduce you to Aidan Sutherland and
Eleanor Sterling.

You met Aidan last year in *An Innocent in Paradise*. He's
the identical twin brother of Logan Sutherland. (And
don't you just love the idea of gorgeous twin brothers?
I know I do.) Like his twin brother, Aidan is wealthy,
powerful and ambitious. He'll never get married because,
first of all, why would he? He's surrounded by gorgeous
women in bikinis at his resort hotel on the Caribbean
island of Alleria. Aidan has other, darker reasons to avoid
starting a family, but when Eleanor Sterling, his senior
vice president, announces that she intends to visit a
fertility clinic to get pregnant, he realizes he may have to
adjust his attitude about such things.

I hope you love Aidan and Ellie's story as much as I loved
writing it. Please let me know! Contact me through my
website at www.katecarlisle.com and while you're there,
be sure to check out the photos and links to the fantasy
resorts I daydreamed about as I wrote this story, as well as
my latest contest info and lots of other fun stuff.

Happy reading!

Kate Carlisle

KATE CARLISLE

SHE'S HAVING THE BOSS'S BABY

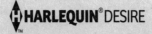

Recycling programs
for this product may
not exist in your area.

ISBN-13: 978-0-373-73240-1

SHE'S HAVING THE BOSS'S BABY

Printed in U.S.A.

www.Harlequin.com

Books by Kate Carlisle

Harlequin Desire

How to Seduce a Billionaire #2104
An Innocent in Paradise #2129
She's Having the Boss's Baby #2227

Silhouette Desire

The Millionaire Meets His Match #2023
Sweet Surrender, Baby Surprise #2058

Other titles by this author available in ebook format.

KATE CARLISLE

New York Times bestselling author Kate Carlisle was born and raised by the beach in Southern California. After more than twenty years in television production, Kate turned to writing the types of mysteries and romance novels she always loved to read. She still lives by the beach in Southern California with her husband, and when they're not taking long walks in the sand or cooking or reading or painting or taking bookbinding classes or trying to learn a new language, they're traveling the world, visiting family and friends in the strangest places. Kate loves to hear from readers. Visit her website at www.katecarlisle.com.

This book is fondly dedicated
to my smart and talented friend Jurene Hogan,
one of the great romance readers of the world.

One

"What else can go wrong today?"

Aidan Sutherland stared at the latest cryptic email from his foreman on the nearby construction site and swore. Usually, Aidan let stuff like this slide right off him. Despite his power and wealth, he prided himself on his easygoing nature and smooth ability to roll with the punches. It wasn't like him to complain or whine about an unexpected setback.

But this latest problem was number fifty-seven in a whole list of complications and snafus that had cropped up today. And hell, it wasn't even lunchtime. Enough was enough.

He read the foreman's message over again and confirmed that as far as problems went, this one wasn't too earth shattering. Aidan would need to get it taken care of within twenty-four hours though, so he would have to re-prioritize a few agenda items and shift some man power, and the issue would be solved. No sweat.

"So why am I sweating it?" Irritated with himself, he

shoved his chair back from his desk, stood and crossed the wide expanse of his penthouse office suite to the wall of windows. As he stared out at the lavish grounds of the gorgeous Alleria Resort that spread out in all directions, his irritation slowly dissolved and satisfaction rose up in its place.

With a quiet laugh, Aidan thought back to the days when this island paradise had been little more than a pipe dream. As youngsters, he and his twin brother, Logan, had plotted and dreamed of becoming like one of their comic book superheroes. Iron Man, maybe, or Batman, with wealth and power beyond imagination. If they could wangle a superhero talent like X-ray vision, that would be a bonus. But above all, their imaginary scheme involved amassing a vast empire, and for two California kids who were swimming before they could walk, what would better serve as their empire headquarters than a remote tropical island? They would conduct business from a couple of hammocks under a shady coconut palm tree.

Aidan watched as a catamaran set sail from the marina below. He and Logan had pretty much achieved the dream— although their hammock and palm tree headquarters had been traded in for several large suites at the Alleria Resort Hotel. Not bad for two working-class guys who'd spent much of their youth surfing and partying.

For several of those years, the brothers had been lucky enough to sweep most of the surfing competitions they'd taken part in. They'd managed to collect enough prize money to finally fulfill the promise they'd made to their father years before. More than anything else, Dad had wanted them both to go to college.

No one was more surprised than Aidan and Logan when they were accepted to one of the most elite universities on the East Coast. While there, as legend had it, they'd won the deed to their first bar in a fraternity poker game.

Aidan and Logan had also excelled in all their classes, graduated with highest honors, and gone on to collect MBA degrees. But those dry facts had little or no entertainment value, so these days, most business magazine articles featuring the Sutherland brothers chose to highlight their misspent youth by recounting sordid tales of surfing, gambling and partying.

Aidan and his brother didn't really care what the articles claimed. The truth was that they had succeeded beyond their wildest dreams through a capricious combination of business acumen, poker winnings, surfing philosophy, sweat and hard work. Added to all that was some good timing and a hell of a lot of dumb luck, and the result was the present-day empire known as Sutherland Corporation. Now their lavish bars and exclusive resorts could be found in every part of the world, including their very own island, Alleria.

They were living the dream.

The Alleria Resort had become the number-one destination for discerning travelers the world over. It also doubled as the headquarters of Sutherland Corporation. And thanks to the brothers' stewardship, the entire island of Alleria was now a bustling, thriving port of call in the Caribbean.

Aidan returned to his desk and grabbed his coffee mug. While he refilled it from the coffeemaker on the sideboard, he thought about his twin brother. Logan was currently in Europe on his honeymoon with his bride, Grace.

"That's why everything's been going wrong lately," he realized aloud. "Too many weddings."

Once the happy couple returned, things would get back to normal around here, Aidan thought. *Well, not right away,* he amended. Because speaking of weddings, his own father would be taking the plunge soon, too. Aidan shook his head. As if he wasn't already surrounded by enough blissful love-birds to mess up his mojo for years to come!

He couldn't begrudge Dad and his beloved Sally their nuptials, though. The two had found each other after years of living alone, so Aidan was happy for them. Still, all of his problems had seemed to start around the same time that everyone began to get happy and fall in love.

Dad and Sally had decided to conduct the ceremony right here on Alleria next month, so that was one more item that needed to be coordinated. In the meantime, Aidan was scheduled to fly to California this coming weekend to take care of some legal business that had to be finalized before Dad married Sally Duke.

"Damn." He'd forgotten to get started on those documents for his father. What the hell? It wasn't like Aidan to forget something like that. Was he losing his grip? Hell no, but he *had* lost his secretary. She'd abandoned him to marriage, too. Just when he'd needed her most, his trusted ally had fallen in love and gone off to Jamaica to marry her sweetheart. Why did the woman have to quit the same week Logan left town?

At the risk of repeating himself, what was the deal with all these weddings lately?

All that creeping happiness had begun to close in on him and he was pretty certain it had caused the balance of nature to shift. The end result was that Aidan kept forgetting stuff. It made an odd sort of sense, really. Aidan would never in a million years have anything to do with the state of matrimony himself, and yet here he was, surrounded by weddings. It was downright bizarre. No wonder Aidan had taken his eye off the ball. Everything in his carefully organized world was going up in smoke lately.

He pulled out his smartphone and compared his electronic calendar with the written schedule he kept on his desk, checking to see if anything else had fallen by the wayside lately. Ordinarily, he was on top of every single detail of Sutherland Corporation business, but as he checked his calendar, he noted that since Logan's wedding a week ago, he'd allowed a few things to drift. They wouldn't cause any major problems, but that didn't excuse his forgetfulness.

The Erickson deal, he noted, would have to be handled within the next three weeks. With Logan away on his honeymoon, Aidan decided to hand the project off to Ellie. He'd been doing that a lot lately, he admitted to himself, but only because he was knee deep in other plans and strategy involving the boutique hotel the Duke brothers were about to break ground on a few miles away on the north shore of the island. The Dukes were his cousins and were experts at negotiating with the unions, but they weren't here on the island. Not yet, anyway.

And frankly, Ellie would handle the deal better. While there were no better negotiators on earth than Aidan and Logan, Ellie brought an extra touch of nuance to any discussion. She could handle Erickson, the union bosses and the Dukes with no problem, he thought. Not that he would pile all that on her, but the fact was, if she was in charge, they'd get done. Clearly, with all that was going on, Aidan had to admit he couldn't depend entirely on his own memory right now.

As a rule, Aidan thrived on meticulous attention to detail. And didn't that sound like he walked around with a giant stick up his ass? He didn't. He was cool, calm and laid-back at all times, damn it. An easygoing guy. But he still expected things to run smoothly and he paid his well organized team a lot of money to make sure they always did.

"Knock, knock."

"What?" he demanded, whipping around to glare at whoever was here to aggravate him.

"Ooh, not a good time?"

"Ellie." Aidan relaxed instantly at the sight of Eleanor

Sterling, his senior vice president, standing at his office door. "Come in. Sorry I barked at you."

"Something not going smoothly?"

"Nothing that can't be fixed," he said. "A little mix-up over at the construction site, but we'll work it out. In fact, you're just the person I wanted to talk to about it. But you go first. What's on your mind?"

"I have a list of things to go over with you," she said, holding up the small, sleek computer tablet that was never out of her sight.

"Of course you do," he murmured, chuckling. When had their super-efficient, proactive, forward-thinking senior vice president ever *not* had a list?

Even when his world was tipping crazily out of balance, he could count on Ellie to be exactly who she was. His ruthlessly organized, efficient right-hand man. Woman. Person.

Ellie approached his desk and Aidan's breath got caught somewhere in his throat as he watched her plant herself in the chair opposite him and cross her stunning long legs.

Damn. He turned away to stare at…something else. This had been happening a lot lately and it was one more thing he could blame on all that wedding madness. Or it would be, if it weren't for the fact that he'd been ogling his business associate's legs for a long time now. Every time she came near him lately, he was ready to pounce like a jungle cat. And who could blame him? The woman had world-class legs. And a world-class smile. He was pretty sure she had world-class breasts, as well, but that was none of his business. She had a gorgeous smile and beautiful lips. Clear blue eyes, an adorable nose and lush dark hair that she wore in a straight style that fell like a thick ribbon halfway down her back.

Was this attraction to Ellie one more example of the sneaky universe conspiring to ruin his life? Was there such a thing as orange-blossom poisoning? Had he overdosed on weddings? Absolutely. That's all this was. Too much romance and talk of happy ever after. So of course he'd been noticing Ellie's legs lately. He'd have been blind not to.

There, a perfectly reasonable explanation. He felt better. Except for the knot of need in his stomach and the more *visible* sign of his desire that he fought to suppress before she noticed and ran screaming from his office.

After a long moment, he turned and gave her a nonchalant smile, as if he hadn't been picturing her naked in his bed seconds ago. But hell, a jury of his peers would never blame him for having those thoughts. She was wearing a dress in some cheery, summery color that was sleeveless and short and contoured to fit her well-endowed body perfectly. When had she started dressing so… *Hmm.* Had she always been this sexy and he just hadn't noticed until recently? Damn. Might be time to get his eyes checked, after all.

Whatever, that dress showed off her smooth, lightly tanned arms and her aforementioned awesomely hot legs.

And now that he thought about it, he realized Ellie rarely wore dresses, preferring lightweight tailored suits and what Aidan referred to as "sensible" shoes. But the weather had turned even warmer than usual lately and they did live and work on a tropical island, after all. That might explain those three-inch-high strappy sandals she wore that gave even more definition to her attractively toned legs.

He mentally kicked his ass. Thinking of his senior VP like this was completely unacceptable. The woman brought incredible resourcefulness and negotiating talent to the company. Not sex. Not ever. End of story.

He blamed his wayward thoughts on the fact that he hadn't been out with a woman in… How long had it been? Didn't matter. Ellie was off-limits. He reeled in his urges, sat down at his desk and smiled tightly at Ellie. "So what can I do to you?"

"Excuse me?" she said.

"I mean, do *for* you?" Good grief. "Sorry, I'm a little distracted by that, uh, union issue I mentioned. So what's on your list?"

As she studied the tablet screen, she wriggled in her chair, uncrossed and re-crossed her legs. Aidan was captivated by the movement and wondered if she would mind if he pulled her onto his desk and began to lick every inch of her legs, starting with her ankles and moving up to her—

"Number one on the agenda has to do with the new sports center," Ellie said. "The Paragon contracts are printed and ready to sign."

With his jaw clenched, Aidan forced the sultry image away and shook himself back to attention. Now what was she saying? Oh, yeah. Paragon was the vendor that would be supplying the center with everything from workers' uniforms to gym towels to drinking cups. Aidan and Logan were old surfing buddies with Keith Sands, the Paragon CEO, and knew him well.

"Good," Aidan said. "Let's overnight them to Keith and get that wrapped up."

"Done." She tapped out a message on her screen keyboard, then nibbled on her bottom lip as she studied the screen. Aidan tortured himself by watching her luscious mouth in action and wondered if maybe he needed to take a cold shower.

As he dragged his gaze away, he vowed to find himself a date while visiting California over the weekend. It had been too long since he'd indulged in some good old-fashioned, no-strings-attached sex. That had to be another reason why he was so distracted by Ellie's excellent body, but he had to snap out of it. There was no way he would allow the one-way attraction to grow. Otherwise, he would never shake off this funk. "What's next?"

She pressed the tablet's surface and a new screen appeared. Glancing up, she said, "As you know, the new hotel is on track to break ground in two weeks."

"Right. But there's a holdup with the cement mixer company."

"Yes, I spoke to them," Ellie said. "I think we've worked it out. I'll keep you posted."

"Thanks, I appreciate you taking on that issue. Next agenda item?" Aidan asked.

"Right. This one's a little tricky." She shook her hair back and took a deep breath. "I'm overdue for some time off and I'm sorry for the short notice, but I have to take three weeks off next month, from the second to the twenty-third." She checked her tablet. "I've arranged coverage for all of my assignments so there shouldn't be any problems."

Before Aidan could say a word, Ellie rushed on to the next item on her list. "Now this is good news, but I'll need you to approve it. The hotel's limousine service will upgrade their entire fleet six weeks from now. I've worked out a deal with a company over on St. Bart's to buy the old cars, but we'll need to ship them there by freighter. They're willing to split the freight cost, but I'd rather we be the ones to arrange everything. There's a new Danish shipping company based in Nassau that can do it, but I'll have to let them know fairly soon if we're interested in using them."

"Send me their info and I'll get back to you." He held up his finger to stop her from continuing. "But...let's go back to that last item you mentioned."

"The cement mixer?" she asked, her eyes wide and curious.

He didn't believe that wide-eyed innocent act for a second. "No, Ellie. Your vacation. Three weeks?"

"Yes, but don't worry. I don't leave until next month."

He grabbed his calendar and calculated the dates. "We're

practically at the end of this month. So next month starts next week. You want to leave a week from tomorrow?"

"Yes. Something important just came up. I'm sorry I couldn't give you more notice, but it's urgent that I go."

He frowned at the calendar. "A week from tomorrow?"

"Yes, a week from tomorrow." She said the words slowly, as though she was speaking to a recalcitrant kindergartner.

"That's really short notice."

"I know, Aidan. But I have an important appointment scheduled and the timing is crucial. I have to leave a week from tomorrow."

His eyes widened. "Is something wrong, Ellie? Are you sick?"

"No!" she said at once. "No, I'm fine. But this can't be put off."

"I'm glad it's nothing health-related." He flipped through the week-at-a-glance calendar. "But can't we talk about this? I really need you on the job over the next month or so. You know I'm about to leave for a long weekend. And Logan won't be back for two more weeks. The Erickson deal needs immediate attention, the Duke project needs supervision, and I've got a dozen new secretary applicants I was hoping you'd help me interview. I hate to be hard-nosed about this, but it's really a bad time for you to be gone."

"No, it's not. I've worked out the—"

"Wait," he said, ignoring her as he tapped the calendar page. "The cardboard-box convention is right in the middle of that time period. That's your client. Those guys love you. You can't desert them."

"I'm not. I'm leaving them in good hands. They love our sales staff."

"It's not the same," he said, grasping at excuses. Damn it, he was already without his secretary. How the hell could he keep this place running without Ellie, as well? "You know you have a knack with the conventioneers." He peered at her. What was this sudden vacation all about? Was she planning to meet up with some man? Aidan wasn't sure he liked the idea, not that he had any say in the matter. Of course, that had never stopped him from issuing an opinion. "What's so important that you need to go next week?"

She gazed back at him steadily. "It's personal."

"You can tell me. We're friends."

"You're my boss."

"And your friend."

She smiled. "Trust me, Aidan. You don't want to know."

He folded his hands together on his desk and smiled patiently. "Now that's where you're wrong. What can possibly be so important that you can only give one week's notice and then go off and leave us for three long weeks? We need you here."

"I appreciate that, but I'm entitled to a vacation."

"Of course you are," he said, wondering why he was being so inflexible about this. She was their best employee. Employee? Hell, she was practically a partner in the business. Of course she was entitled to take time off. He just didn't want her to leave right now while things were in flux. It was bad enough he didn't have a secretary. But to lose his right-hand man—er, *woman*—for three weeks? He didn't want to think of the many things that could go wrong. "We have two major construction projects going, there are union issues, my brother is out of the country, I'm going to have to travel, as well. You know we depend on you to keep everything running smoothly."

"But—"

"It's not about whether you *deserve* the time off," he rushed to add. "It's just that, hell, you're always so organized. You plan your vacation time a year in advance. What happened?"

"Something came up," she said primly.

"Damn it, Ellie. What in the world is so important that you'd leave five hundred convention attendees in the lurch?" *Not to mention me,* he didn't say aloud.

She let go an exasperated sigh, then said, "Fine. But don't say I didn't warn you." She bounded out of her chair and paced back and forth in front of his desk. Suddenly she stopped and said in a rush, "I have an appointment with a fertility clinic in Atlanta. The timing is critical because everything depends on my ovulation cycle. Once I arrive in Atlanta, the clinic advised that I'll need two days of complete rest to get over any jet lag my ovaries might suffer. Then it'll take a week to go through their process, and that's followed up with two weeks of, well, rest and waiting."

Aidan's eyes widened. He shook his head. Had his ears plugged up suddenly? He couldn't have heard what he thought he'd just heard. *Ovaries?* Good grief. *Fertility?*

He glared at her. "What in the world are you talking about?"

Wearing a serene smile now, Ellie sat back down in her chair. "I'm going to have a baby."

There. She had finally said it out loud.

Ellie tried to appear calm, tried not to squirm in her chair as Aidan stared sharply at her. Well, it was his own darn fault for pushing the point, she thought. Honestly, she had tried to soft-peddle her vacation plans, tried to avoid explaining all the gory details, but she should've known Aidan Sutherland wouldn't let things slide. He never let things slide.

Yes, she usually planned her vacations a year ahead of time. Yes, she was highly organized, detail oriented, never impulsive, always in control. She didn't do anything without preparing a spreadsheet first. But come on, once in a while a girl had to be spontaneous. That's what she'd heard, anyway. Ellie was pretty sure she'd never been spontaneous in her life. Until now.

She watched Aidan's gaze narrow in on her. He turned his head slightly and leaned forward, almost as though he'd experienced a hearing loss. "Say that again?"

Ellie sighed. She and Aidan had a fabulous working relationship. She thought of him as her best friend at work, even though he was her boss. And even though he was rugged and gregarious, athletic and tanned. And gorgeous. Handsome. Downright sexy. But she was getting off track.

The fact was, she'd liked Aidan from the first day she started her job at Sutherland Corp. The two of them shared a lot of the same interests and as business associates, they'd traveled together on dozens of occasions. Together they had closed numerous deals and even a bar or two when the negotiations turned out to be rougher than they should have been.

It didn't help that she had developed a ridiculous schoolgirl crush on Aidan shortly after she started working with him. It didn't matter though, because she would never do anything so stupid as to act on her feelings. Not only would it destroy their relationship and mark the end of the best job she'd ever had, but it would make her feel like the world's biggest fool. Ellie had never been a fool.

She knew Aidan's question was coming from a decent place inside him, and she had already decided to be completely honest with him if he forced the issue, so she repeated, "I said, I'm going to have a baby."

"Next week?"

"Next week is when the process starts."

"You can't put it off an extra week?"

"No," she said, fighting to maintain her calm. "I'm usually as regular as clockwork so once I get to Atlanta, I've allowed myself a three-day window during which I should start ovula—"

"Stop." He held up his hand. "We're venturing back into the dark realm of too much female information."

"But you keep asking."

"I just want to know why you have to do all this starting next week."

"Because I want to have a baby and I'm not getting any younger." She had no intention of telling him anything more than that.

"But—" He scratched his head, clearly confused. "You're going to a sperm bank."

"I prefer the term fertility clinic. But yes, that's where I'm going."

"But why?"

"Why?" she said, her voice rising as her serenity tottered on the edge of annoyance. "Seriously, Aidan? You want to know why I'm going to a sperm bank— I mean, fertility clinic? I'll go out on a limb here and take a guess that you are aware of what happens in those places."

He huffed impatiently. "Of course. But what I mean is, why don't you just do it the old-fashioned way?"

"Oh," she said slowly. "That."

"Yeah." He folded his arms across his chest. "That."

"Well, it's because… Hmm." What was she supposed to tell him? The truth? Because the truth was that she would have preferred to get pregnant the old-fashioned way. With a man she loved, someone wonderful who wanted to live the rest of his life with her.

Recently there had been one man who'd expressed some interest in her. She had dated him for a few weeks, but as soon as Ellie brought up the subject of children and family, he'd made himself scarce. That was before they'd even had sex so she'd missed out on that, too. She just couldn't get a break.

Even though there were plenty of opportunities to meet

eligible men on the island, none of them ever seemed to want to take the next step. One problem was that most men came to Alleria to party-party-party. They weren't interested in a relationship if it looked like it might last more than a week.

The other problem was that while Ellie knew men thought she was pretty enough, she also knew they found her a little intimidating. And even though she recognized the problem, she didn't know what to do about it. It wasn't that she had an overpowering personality. That would've been an easy fix. No, Ellie's problem was that she was just too smart. She couldn't help it. She seemed to have a photographic memory and she loved learning new things. She retained information and was cheerfully willing to share it with others any time a subject came up. Some people didn't take that well.

And sadly, Ellie didn't have a clue when to keep her mouth shut and let a guy live with the illusion that he was smarter than she was. Men were so odd.

These days, though, Ellie refused to allow that to bother her. Happily, Aidan and his brother appreciated how smart she was and she loved her job because of it. They accepted her and needed her, and that meant a lot more to Ellie than having a man in her life who might cause her to lose too much of herself.

But meanwhile, without a man in her life, there was no one who was willing to make a baby with her.

So after a lot of studying the pros and cons and debating it with herself, she had decided to use artificial insemination to achieve her goal of motherhood.

She was secure in her job and very well compensated. She also had an excellent benefits package, so the idea of raising her child on her own was a reasonable one. She was also lucky to have developed strong friendships with several women on the island, too, and knew they would always be around when she needed them. So she wasn't worried. She and her baby would comprise the perfect little family she had always wanted. Now she just needed some time off to get the job done.

"Ellie, are you going to tell me why you can't just do it the—"

"Yes, yes, the old-fashioned way." She sniffed, straightened her shoulders and held her head high. "I don't think it's any of your business."

"You're probably right." His lips twisted in a sardonic grin. "But you've already given me your ovulation schedule. I mean, why hold back the rest?"

"Oh, for Pete's sake," Ellie said. "Look, we both know that what I do in my free time is nobody's business but my own."

"Of course it is," he said reasonably. "But you have to realize how concerned I am. As I've already said, I'm your friend as well as your employer, and this isn't exactly a vacation you're taking. You're planning to go off to get pregnant. And then what happens? Then you'll come back and work? For how long?"

"Until the baby's born," she said immediately. "At that point I'll take maternity leave for three months and then I'll be back at work."

The resort had an excellent childcare facility so Ellie wasn't worried about finding someone to care for her baby while she worked. That was another benefit of working for the Sutherland brothers.

"Three months." Aidan pushed away from the desk and stood to pace the floor for a full minute. Finally he looked at her. "Okay, I'm not going to think about your being gone for three months. We'll just deal with these upcoming three weeks."

"That might be best," she murmured.

"I can't stand in the way of you going, but what will we do without you for three weeks? It might not sound like a lot of time to you, but we've never gone that long without you before. And right now we're swamped with work and no one else is qualified to fill your shoes."

She smiled because she'd already made a point of finding solutions to those particular problems, thanks to her best friend, Serena, the catering manager.

"Serena and her secretary have agreed to assist the sales force with the convention work. And my secretary will take care of making sure the day-to-day office work gets done. I'll be available by phone if there are any questions."

"Damn, Ellie."

She stood and met him face-to-face. "Look, Aidan. I wouldn't leave if there was a doctor on the island who specialized in fertilization. But there isn't, so I'm going to Atlanta."

"But what if you go through all this and it doesn't…" He seemed to weigh his words and decided not to finish that sentence. Probably smart of him.

She finished the thought for him. "What if the procedure doesn't work?" She'd considered that possibility, too. "I'll try again in a few months."

He gritted his teeth. "Okay, I understand what you want to do and it's not like I have a say in your decision, but I still think you're jumping the gun here. You're so young. What are you? Twenty-eight? Twenty-nine?"

"Thirty."

"That's young," he insisted. "You still have plenty of time to do it the—"

"Yes, yes, the old-fashioned way. You've mentioned it several times already."

"It bears repeating," he said amiably.

She quickly looked down at her tablet to avoid his knowing gaze. Was it getting hot in here? All this conversation about babies and "doing it the old-fashioned way" was stirring up feelings for Aidan that she'd long ago squelched. And not just emotional feelings, but an actual physical attraction to him. And that had to stop right now. "You realize this is absolutely none of your business, right?"

He had the nerve to grin. "Yeah."

She sighed again. "Look, even if I do have plenty of time, I don't have a partner. You know, someone who's interested in providing the necessary equipment to get the job done."

Could she make it any clearer than that?

"Oh. Right." Aidan seemed to ponder that for a moment. "But what about that guy you were dating? Aren't you still seeing him? What's his name?"

"You know very well what his name is," she said drily. "You introduced us, remember?"

"Oh, yeah," he said snidely. "Brad."

"Blake," she said, rolling her eyes. "Blake Farrell."

"Right. What about Blake?"

Self-conscious now, Ellie avoided eye contact. "What about Blake for what?"

Aidan raised one eyebrow, but said nothing.

"Oh, fine," she said, exasperated. She knew exactly what he was referring to. Sex. "If you must know, I'm not seeing Blake anymore."

His mouth opened, then closed. After a pause, he said, "Ah. Sorry it didn't work out."

"You don't sound sorry at all."

"You're right." He grinned wolfishly. "I'm not. He wasn't the guy for you."

"But you introduced me to him."

"You were both standing there," he said with a shrug. "I was just being polite. I never expected you to start dating him. I'm glad you broke up. You can do a lot better than him."

"Now you tell me," she muttered. "After I already asked him to…" She stopped talking, but it was too late.

Aidan's eyes narrowed in on her. "You asked him to be the father of your child?"

"I think this conversation has gone far enough." She grabbed her tablet off the chair and turned to leave.

"Funny, I think it's just getting started." He circled around to meet her face-to-face, effectively preventing her from dashing out of his office. "Ellie, I introduced you to Blake three weeks ago. Are you saying that after three weeks of dating, you asked him to—"

"Yes. Yes, I did." She began pacing again, but couldn't get far with him standing right in front her. "I don't know what I was thinking. But in my defense, we were going out every weekend, having a great time, getting to know each other. So one night at dinner he asked me where I saw myself in five years and I told him."

"You told him what, exactly?"

She wanted to bury herself somewhere. Instead, she drew in a breath and said, "I told him that in five years I saw myself living on Alleria, working for Sutherland Corporation, and taking care of my adorable four-year-old child."

She watched Aidan's eyes widen. His lips quivered. He tried to bite back a grin, but it was useless. He finally began to laugh. "Let me get this straight. You basically told a guy you've been dating for three weeks that you're looking for him to be your baby daddy?"

"Not exactly," she said. But it was no use. His laughter was justified. "Okay, he might've interpreted it that way."

"You think?"

"Stop laughing. What do I know? Blake was the first date I've had in three years."

"Three years?" He looked her up and down. "What's wrong with the guys you know?"

"It's not them, it's me." Oh, dear lord. Could she sound like a bigger loser? She had to get out of there.

But Aidan grabbed her shoulders to keep her there and tilted his head to meet her gaze. "Honey, trust me. It's not you. You're smart, funny, beautiful. Any man would… well…" He faltered, frowning as he let go of her.

She blinked up at him, then frowned, too. "Well, what?"

He scowled as he walked back to his desk. "Just trust me. You're not the problem."

Ellie appreciated his words, but they didn't really help right now. It wasn't much fun admitting that she was a total loser when it came to men. Especially to admit it to Aidan Sutherland, who was not only her boss but also the man she had been crushing on for almost four years.

Not that it meant anything. A crush on a man was healthy, right? Of course it was! Sure, she had a personal hang-up or two, but other than wanting to sleep with her boss, she was fine and dandy. Very put-together, highly organized, successful. She had friends. She wasn't a loser.

She smiled with determination. "I'll say again that I'm sorry I couldn't give you more notice, but I've got everything covered job-wise. I am absolutely certain that things will run smoothly. I just need your blessing to take the time off."

"I won't let you quit your job," he said fiercely. "We need you too much."

She was surprised and delighted by his admission. He had no idea how much his words pleased her, but she was still going through with her plan.

"Aidan, you know me. I love my job. I love Alleria. You and Logan are the best people I've ever worked with. Believe me, I've never been happier and I have no intention of ever leaving voluntarily."

"Good, because I won't let you. You're a vital member of our organization."

"Thank you." She wouldn't say it aloud, but she would be a fool to give up this job. After all this time, with all the raises and bonuses they'd given her, she would never find anything comparable, especially in such a beautiful setting as Alleria.

"I'll never leave," she reiterated.

"But you're going to have a baby," he argued, not quite ready to concede. "That's not a good sign."

"I have every intention of raising my baby here on the island and continuing to work for you and Logan for as long as you'll have me. Okay?"

He scowled, but she knew he was smart enough to know when to give up the fight. Finally he nodded. "Okay."

"Thank you," she said. In a spontaneous gesture, she gave him a tight hug. "I really appreciate your understanding."

"I don't understand anything," he said, but managed a half smile as he walked her to the door. "Call me conventional, but I still believe in the man-woman routine."

Her laugh was lighthearted even if her mind was set. But she decided to humor him anyway. "Fine. You have one week to convince me it's the best way to go."

Not that she had any intention of doing things his way, Ellie thought as she walked back to her office. She'd thought this through down to the last detail, and she wasn't about to change her mind just to satisfy her boss. She'd seen how a messy relationship with a man could turn a woman's life inside out and she wasn't about to let that happen to her. Not ever. Not even for Aidan Sutherland.

Two

Later that evening, Aidan sat in one of the resort's plush beach chairs and stared out at the placid surface of Alleria Bay. He nursed the glass of single malt scotch he'd picked up in the bar earlier before wandering out to the beach to relax and enjoy the quiet evening.

But how could he relax? He'd already been thinking about Ellie in all sorts of inappropriate ways, and then she had come along and added to the problem. True, she'd only been talking about babies. It was Aidan's fault for bringing up sex by suggesting that she do it the traditional way. Now he couldn't get the idea of sex with Ellie out of his head.

But that didn't mean he would act on it. No way. He had to get his mind off his associate and he hoped his upcoming trip to California would help.

Realistically, Ellie wanting a baby was none of his business. But as she'd left his office earlier, she had issued the challenge—joking or not—and Aidan was willing to meet it. He was determined to find her a willing man in a week. The Sutherland twins never backed away from a challenge. But how was he supposed to find a decent guy who would make Ellie happy enough to stay on the island where Aidan needed her? It's not like he could approach one of the guys he knew and ask if they would be willing to impregnate his senior vice president.

That would be weird.

Skimming his feet over the cool sand of the beach, Aidan tried to figure out where he'd lost the argument with Ellie. Not that he'd been given much chance to argue, he thought. Ellie had presented her plan as a fait accompli. She had no intention of backing down, and Aidan had to admit he appreciated that quality in her. She'd made the decision and she was sticking to it.

So why in the world was Aidan making such a big deal over it? The choice to have a baby was Ellie's alone to make. It was her life. If she wanted to have a baby, she should go get pregnant and have a baby.

But then she'd be leaving the island. True, it was only for three weeks, but she'd confessed out loud that if the first time didn't work, she'd be going back again. And again.

Aidan hated to admit it, but things never ran as smoothly when Ellie went away. He would even go so far as to say that things tended to go straight to hell when Ellie was gone. Two years ago, she took five days off and Hurricane Willie struck the island. Last year she was gone for a week and the hotel kitchen staff went on strike.

She was like a barometer for all things Alleria. If Ellie was on the island, life rolled along. When she wasn't, it was more of a crash-and-burn scenario.

Aidan was tempted to fly in a fertility specialist if it meant Ellie would stay on the island. He considered that for a second or two. It was the perfect solution. One that would make everybody happy, right?

So why was he still brooding about it?

Because, Aidan thought as he sipped his scotch, it still meant that Ellie would be using artificial means to have a baby. And that was the one thing Aidan refused to accept. He wasn't ready to examine his feelings too closely, but suffice to say it wasn't *fair* that his beautiful senior vice president was choosing to get pregnant by means of a turkey baster.

"Fair?" he muttered aloud. Fair to whom? To Ellie? Or to the male population at large? After all, she was a beautiful woman. Plenty of men would be thrilled to help her out. Had she given any of them a chance? Hell, no.

Even Blake Farrell. She hadn't given him a chance, not really. After all, they'd only been dating for less than a month. What man in his right mind would agree to accept her obvious baby-daddy ploy so quickly after they'd met?

Aidan scowled. The *right* man would. But Blake Farrell wasn't that guy. Aidan had known Blake Farrell for years. The guy was a player. He ran an air-shipping operation over on Nassau and had recently opened an office in the port of Alleria. He'd bought a small house in town so he was part of the island community now.

But if Aidan had thought for one moment that Ellie would start dating Farrell, Aidan never would've introduced the two. It still rankled him that she'd accepted even one date from him.

Blake wasn't right for Ellie and he definitely was not the appropriate choice to be the father of her child. But who was? Not that Aidan had any say in the matter, but if Ellie needed someone to do the job, there had to be a lot of guys better suited for the job than Blake Farrell.

Frankly, although he didn't want to examine his feelings

on the subject too closely, he had been relieved to hear that there was no current man in Ellie's life.

But now that meant that she was going to have a complete *stranger* father her child. She would be picking some guy's description out of a book—and who was to say the guy was telling the truth about his attributes? Anybody could donate sperm and claim to be a six-foot-five Adonis when in reality he was three feet tall and a troglodyte.

Hadn't she considered that? Scowling to himself, Aidan imagined all kinds of weird possibilities stemming from that damn turkey baster.

"Hell, I should offer to do it myself," he muttered as he sipped his scotch. Abruptly he jerked himself upright in his chair. *Whoa.* He did not just say that. He tossed down a serious amount of scotch to drown out the words.

There was no way he would ever knowingly father a child. He'd made that decision years ago after watching his own father struggle as a single parent. Aidan and Logan's mother had left them when the boys were only seven years old. It had been a defining moment in Aidan's life and while he thoroughly enjoyed the pleasure that women provided, he wasn't about to trust one enough to marry her, let alone have a child with her.

He would never risk a child of his experiencing the abandonment he'd gone through himself. And now he realized that this was a big reason why he wasn't happy that Ellie was planning to go through with the pregnancy on her own. She was walking right into a single parent situation with no idea how difficult her life would become. And she wasn't the only one to consider. Her child would go through life without a dad. That wasn't right.

Had Ellie tried hard enough to find a man to father her child?

But then he remembered the look on her face earlier when she'd said, *It's not them, it's me.*

Hell, of course she'd tried to find a partner, but no one had been smart enough to step forward. She'd been so vulnerable while talking about it, Aidan had almost taken her in his arms and kissed away the pain he'd seen in her eyes. But he hadn't done it, thank God. That would have been a huge mistake.

Not that he wouldn't have enjoyed it, he thought as he stood and walked to the water's edge. That wasn't the point. The point was, it was never going to happen.

Too bad. Because now that he was thinking about topics like trust and women and Ellie, in particular, it occurred to him that there was one woman in the world he did actually trust. Ellie. When it came to business, she was scrupulously honest. She always spoke her mind. And she always had his back in any negotiation they entered. She was almost as good a partner in wheeling and dealing as his brother, Logan, was.

Logan had agreed with Aidan that Ellie would make a good junior partner. Before Logan left on his honeymoon, the brothers had decided to offer Ellie the position. The plan was to wait until Logan got back to the island. They'd never brought in another partner before, but they both agreed that there was nobody better for their organization than Ellie. And if they wanted the company to grow even larger, they needed someone else in the top ranks who had her intelligence, business insight and unwavering principles.

And all that had nothing to do with the fact that she was downright sexy and beautiful. He thought again of those amazing legs of hers, pictured them wrapped around his waist with him buried so far inside her, he could feel it.

The carnal image was so vivid, he almost lost his footing. Damn, his mind was wandering down a perilous path and if he wasn't careful, he'd find himself facedown in the sand.

He recovered quickly and drank down a good slug of scotch. The smooth, liquid heat soothed his throat and snapped him out of his wayward thoughts. His wildly active imagination meant nothing in reality. He liked Ellie, would love to take her to bed, but it wouldn't happen. It couldn't.

How the hell could he risk losing Ellie as a business partner if a romantic thing between them didn't work out? Or worse yet, what if he initiated something and she was so offended she quit?

"She wouldn't just quit," he muttered darkly. "She'd punch you in the nose first and *then* quit. Yeah, that's not gonna happen."

Still, he wanted her to be happy.

But apparently, it was going to take having a baby to accomplish that.

"Hell." He rubbed his face, annoyed with himself. If he was being honest, he would have to admit that if Ellie had approached him and asked him to be the father of her child, he would have had a hard time pushing her away. But he absolutely would've turned her down in the end. Wouldn't he? Of course he would've. There was no way he would say yes to something like that. Even if it was Ellie doing the asking.

"Not that she asked you," he groused, then scowled at his own idiotic statement. It was official: he had lost his mind. Exasperated, he swallowed the rest of the scotch and headed back to his suite before he found himself howling at the moon like the rest of the lunatics in the world.

Ellie yawned, then finished the last of her tea and shut down her computer. She should've gone to bed an hour ago, but since she knew she wouldn't sleep anyway, she had spent more time sifting through the family photos her sister, Brenna, had sent from Atlanta. A picture of Brenna with her darling husband, Brian. One of Brenna and Brian with their two adorable children. Various shots of the kids on their new backyard jungle gym. And the latest one, a blurry ultrasound photo of Brenna's unborn baby.

Doctor's pretty sure it's going to be a boy, Brenna had written in the email. Lilah's so excited to have another brother. No annoying little sister to deal with.

Ellie smiled. She could hear Brenna laughing as she wrote those words, since it was Ellie who'd been the annoying little sister Brenna had dealt with all her life. And thank goodness for that, Ellie thought.

Now Brenna had her own wonderful family and Ellie couldn't wait to see them all again. That was another reason she had chosen the Atlanta clinic. She would get to visit with her sister's happy, loving family again.

Ellie and Brenna hadn't always been this happy. Growing up, their mother had been absent most of the time, even when she was sitting in the same room with them. That was what happened when a woman became so obsessed with a man who wanted nothing to do with her. Rather than give any love or attention to her own children, their mother had kept it all inside, saving it up, just in case their father ever returned. Except he never did. He didn't want anything to do with them. He had moved on, found another woman to marry, a woman who gave birth to children he cared for much more than he had ever cared about his first two daughters.

But Ellie's mother never gave up on him, never stopped loving him or chasing him, never stopped pretending that he would come back one day. She was always ready, always perfectly dressed and coifed in case he showed up at the door. She insisted that the girls be ready, too. And in her own subtle way, their mother never stopped blaming Ellie and Brenna for causing him to leave. That is, when she managed to remember that she had two children who needed her.

One day, when the girls and their mother were enjoying a

rare moment of fun at a local hamburger stand, their mother thought she spied their father walking down the sidewalk. She raced outside to catch him, saw the man cross the street and blindly dashed after him. She was struck and killed by a city bus.

It was one of many lessons that Ellie took with her into adulthood. She would never, ever cling to or chase after a man who didn't love her. Ellie wouldn't do to her own child what her mother had done to Ellie and Brenna.

After all, she didn't want to get hit by a bus.

More than that, she refused to allow her self-esteem to be shattered as her mother's had been. Her mother had made a fool of herself over and over again. She had deluded herself for years and, slowly but surely, the delusions had replaced reality. Ellie would never allow that to happen to her.

She carried her teacup over to the sink and rinsed it out. As the water ran, she thought about the tiny creature in her sister's ultrasound photo, silently waiting to be born into a loving family that couldn't wait to greet their newest little member.

Ellie was so excited for Brenna. The two of them had basically raised themselves after their mother died, staying under the radar so that the county wouldn't send Ellie into foster care. How they'd managed it, they still didn't know. But it meant that they were fiercely loyal to each other. Brenna had taught Ellie so much more about life and real love than she'd ever learned from her mother.

One thing Brenna always wished for herself and Ellie was that someday they would each have their own big, boisterous families to love. She imagined how Christmas mornings would be, with their children staring in awe at all the colorful packages under the tree. It would be a noisy, busy, frenzied moment when they all ripped into their presents and shouted out their joy and excitement.

Ellie smiled at the memory. Now that Brenna's dream had come true, now that she had Brian and a wonderful family of her own, Ellie couldn't be happier. They were her family, too.

Brenna always told Ellie that someday it would happen for her, too. She would meet a man who would love her and want to start a family with her. Ellie had thought she could wait for that day. But five days ago, Blake broke up with her—probably a good thing—and the very next day, her sister announced she was having another baby by way of sending the ultrasound photo.

"You're going to be an auntie again!" the email subject line announced gaily.

Gazing at the fuzzy outline of Brenna's third child, Ellie had realized that *someday* might never come for her. She might always be an auntie, never a mom. That's when she'd impulsively made the decision to do something about it. She would go it alone. And she would do it right away, before she could think about it too much and pick apart all the reasons why she shouldn't do it. She phoned the Atlanta fertility clinic that very minute and made the appointment.

So that was done. Now she just had to deal with one more wrinkle in her plan.

Aidan.

As Ellie recalled Aidan's reaction to her news, her cheeks flushed with heat. *Why not do it the old-fashioned way?* he'd asked her. Would it have shocked him to hear her reply, "Are you offering to do the job?"

Yes, it would've shocked him and probably would've ended her career at Sutherland Corporation. It wasn't often that female employees were fired for sexually harassing the male boss, but there was a first time for everything.

Aidan had promised to try and convince her that the time-honored, man-woman route was the way to go, but she doubted he would bring up the subject again. Especially after she'd made her pitiful confession that she didn't even have a man around to do the job for her, so to speak.

If only Aidan had offered his own services.

"Oh, good grief." She felt herself blushing even worse than before. Was she out of her mind? Aidan was her boss, in case she'd forgotten. There was no end to the list of complications and ramifications of having her own boss be the biological father of her child.

Sadly though, her biggest problem had nothing to do with the fact that Aidan was her boss. It had to do with the fact that she had wanted the man for years. Secretly, of course. She hadn't dwelled on her feelings for him in a long time, and she blamed their discussion about babies and sex for making her think of it now. Except for that conversation, she considered her crush on him mainly shallow and, well, sexual. Nothing wrong with that, right? The man had a great body! He was smart and funny and nice, too. God help her if she ever began to obsess over him, because if her feelings deepened, she would be in big trouble. Hadn't her mother gone through life pining over a man, worshiping him from afar and losing herself in the process?

No, Ellie would never become dependent on a man. She liked Aidan, thought he was sexy, but that was it, thank goodness. There was no way she would ever turn into her mother.

"Hell, no," she muttered defiantly as her hands rolled into fists at the very idea. She tossed her lightweight bathrobe on the bed and climbed under the covers. But as she fluffed her pillow, she wondered what it said about her when, despite the fact that Aidan would never make the offer to get her pregnant, she knew that if he did, she would have a hard time rejecting the offer. No matter how hard she had tried to avoid the attraction she felt for him, a direct proposition would be too tempting to pass up.

"Because you are crazy," she said aloud. But that didn't seem to matter as she continued to reflect on the joys of giving birth to a baby boy whose father was Aidan Sutherland. Her child would grow up to be handsome, rugged, gregarious, smart and athletic, just like his daddy.

She sighed. And even though it would never happen, the thought was so pleasant that she continued to dwell on it as she drifted off to sleep.

Two days later, Aidan held his regular weekly meeting with the resort managers to go over the schedule for the weekend and discuss any problems that might follow them into the next week.

Once the meeting ended, Serena, his catering manager, and Marianne, the head of housekeeping, met at the coffee machine. Aidan waited behind them as the two women filled their mugs and chatted.

"I'll bet she's already packed," Marianne said. She kept her voice low, but she couldn't disguise her excitement. "You know how she is."

"Yes, organized to the teeth," Serena said as she poured a dollop of cream into her cup. "God, I'm going to miss her so much."

"She'll only be gone for three weeks."

"Oh, come on," Serena said quietly. "Once she gets pregnant, do you really think she'll stay?"

"She promised she would."

"But she'll have a baby to take care of."

"Duh," Marianne said. "But she loves it here."

"Of course, who doesn't? But come on, what kind of life will she have trying to raise a child on Alleria?"

"Hello?" Marianne said. "I have two kids and I live here quite nicely, thank you."

Serena slapped her arm lightly. "I know, goofball, but you got yourself a husband first."

Her friend frowned. "True. Hmm."

"If Ellie's determined to have a baby, she'll want a husband eventually and she's sure not going to find one here."

Marianne sighed. "I have to agree with you there. The men who come to Alleria are only looking for short-term action."

Serena gazed at her. "And yet you found Hector here."

"Sure did," Marianne said, winking as she rolled her shoulder seductively. "He came here looking for one hot mama and he found her."

They both giggled and Serena said, "You got lucky and so did Hector. But the last thing most men come here for is a mama, no matter how hot she is."

"I guess you're right," Marianne said. "It breaks my heart."

"Mine, too, but Ellie will soon realize her child needs a father." Serena leaned closer. "Remember I told you about my sister being a single mother? She's struggled for years just to get by. It's not right."

Marianne sighed. "Alleria is no place for a single mother to go looking for a father for her child."

The two women continued to chat as they walked away, never looking back to notice Aidan's stricken look. He gazed at their backs until they disappeared into the hall. Then he sat down and thought about what he'd heard.

Those women were two of Ellie's best friends on the island. If they expected her to leave, how could Aidan expect anything different?

That settled it. He had weighed all the options and there was only one clear way forward. Serena and Marianne were right. Aidan couldn't take the chance that Ellie would realize she'd need to leave the island once she was raising her child on her own. He had to take action. He'd been tossing ideas around for the last three days and it was driving him crazy. But after hearing what those women had said, he knew there was only one solution.

Now he just had to convince Ellie.

"No. No way. Absolutely not," Ellie said as she jumped up from her chair and faced him. "Are you crazy?"

Maybe he was, Aidan thought. When this same thought had occurred to him a few days ago, he'd dismissed it out of hand as a sure sign he was losing his mind. But after he'd overheard that conversation yesterday, he'd reconsidered and now this seemed the most logical solution to his problem. He could give Ellie a baby. They could do it the old-fashioned way. One problem solved.

"More importantly," he continued, ignoring her protests. "I could support the child and you. You wouldn't have to worry about being a single mother. It's the best possible solution to the problem."

"I don't have a problem," she countered.

"Not yet, maybe. But look at what this would mean in the short run. You wouldn't have to travel back and forth and worry about getting jet lag, you know, in your ovaries."

She whipped around. "Seriously, Aidan? Jet lag in my ovaries?"

"Hey, I'm just repeating what you said." He shook his head, knowing he sounded ridiculous. But it was too late to turn back now. "And another thing. On the off chance that the injections don't take the first few times, you wouldn't have to drag yourself back and forth from Atlanta."

She didn't say anything in response, but he could tell she was thinking about that one.

"Plus, you can stay here on the island," he pointed out

reasonably, "as you said you'd prefer to do. Plus, I'm right here to support you through it all."

"Uh-huh," she said softly.

"I did some reading," he continued. "There's often a lot of anxiety attached to this whole process. You need to be careful or you could sabotage yourself. You know, you could make yourself infertile or something."

"First, you're nuts," she said, counting off with her fingers. "And second, you did some reading? That's so sweet."

He shrugged. "I'm your friend. I'm concerned."

"You're my boss. You don't want me to go."

"That's secondary," he insisted so strongly he almost convinced himself. "Your health and well-being are my main concern."

She rolled her eyes. "Right. Look, I appreciate it and everything, but your idea would never work."

He leaned closer. "Why, Ellie?"

She gazed back at him intently. "Because you don't want a child."

"But you do."

"Yes, and I have a perfectly sensible and practical way to make it happen. And it doesn't have anything to do with you."

He drew a breath and changed tactics. "We've known each other a long time, right? We get along great. And hey, we're in the same vicinity. So if you were, you know, ovulating and, you know, the time was right, all you'd have to do is call me and I'd be there for you."

"You make it sound so romantic," she said, patting her heart wryly.

"What? A turkey baster in some clinic is more romantic?" He chuckled. "Besides, this isn't about romance, right? It's about the baby you want. And it's about your child knowing who his father is. Don't you want that for him?"

"Him?"

"Ellie," he said, "just think about it. This makes a lot of sense. I can have our lawyers write up a contract that spells out the terms for child support and whatever else you want it to say."

She blinked at that. After a moment, she said, "I'm not sure I want you obligated to support my child."

He'd never met a woman who didn't want his money, but Ellie wasn't like any other woman he'd ever known. He was still determined to provide support, though, but right now the exact terms didn't matter. What mattered was that she would have the baby she wanted. And she would stay and continue to work for Sutherland, which Aidan wanted. And the deal would be done.

Just to be sure they were on the same page, he said, "I would want a clause that says you and the baby will stay and live on Alleria."

"I always planned to do that."

"But you might change your mind after the baby's born."

She shook her head. "I won't."

"You never know," he argued. "You might want to get married someday."

"I have no intention of getting married," she insisted.

"You never know," he said with a shrug. "And if you changed your mind, how would you meet a man around here? Let's face it, most men who come to Alleria are only looking for short-term action."

She gave him a suspicious look and he wondered if her girlfriends had already mentioned that point to her. Didn't matter. The more points he racked up for his side, the better.

As she sat back down in the chair opposite his desk, she nibbled at her lower lip, clearly nervous. Instantly, his groin strained with arousal and all he knew was that if she kept biting those lush lips of hers, he wouldn't be responsible for his actions.

He was getting more and more fond of this whole idea by the minute.

"I'm pretty sure this is a bad idea," she said.

He adjusted himself before leaning forward and resting his arms on his desk. "It's actually a really good idea, Ellie. Unless…" He frowned at her. "Here I've been assuming all this time that you found me attractive enough to go through with it. Maybe I was wrong."

"Oh, don't be ridiculous," she grumbled. "Of course I find you attractive. You're the most… Oh, never mind. You're just fishing for compliments. I refuse to feed your ego."

"Too late." Aidan couldn't help grinning.

"Look," she said after taking a deep breath and letting it out slowly. "This has nothing to do with whether I think you look like a troll or whatever."

"A troll? Thank you."

"I'm kidding. You're not a troll and you know it." Her smile turned sober. "It's just that I find the whole idea a little awkward, that's all."

"Awkward?"

"Well, yeah, Aidan. To do this, we'd have to be *naked*." She blew out a breath. "We work together. Seeing each other, you know…that's awkward."

Naked. Okay, maybe he was just being a guy here, but the only thing he found awkward about this situation was that she wasn't naked *now.* Still…he sat back and thought about what she'd said for a moment. Basically, she felt awkward and it was all his fault. Hell, if he could kick his own ass, he would do it. "Damn, Ellie. I didn't mean to make you uncomfortable."

Now she looked contrite. "It's okay. I know you didn't set

out to embarrass me or anything. It's not in your nature to be mean. But you have to admit the idea's a little…bizarre."

He took a careful sip of coffee and wondered if his desperation was starting to show. He had overplayed his hand and she was about to turn him down. A woman. Turning him down. Was there an apocalypse about to happen that no one had told him about? Logan would laugh his ass off if he ever found out about this conversation.

"You're right," he said wearily. "The last thing I ever wanted to do was hurt our working relationship. If it's possible, can you please forget I ever said anything?"

"Just give me a minute," she murmured.

"Take all the time you need. In fact, if you'd rather collect your thoughts and meet later…"

But she ignored him as she started to voice her feelings. "It makes a certain kind of sense to stay here on the island and take care of it, I mean, do…*it*…with you." She rushed to add, "Even though it's a terrible idea. Because, you know, it's you and me. We're pals. Or we were. I hope we still are. But more than that, you're my boss and I'm your…you know. Your employee. So that makes it a really bad idea, right?"

Truly desperate now, Aidan played what he hoped was his trump card. "What if you were more than my employee? What if I told you I was planning to make you a partner?"

She didn't react right away and Aidan thought maybe she hadn't heard him. He wasn't going to mention the fact that he and Logan had already decided to offer Ellie the partnership. She deserved it and it was past time they offered it to her. And if a partnership deal would help sway her to accept his other offer, he was willing to add it to the pot. On the other hand, if his other offer was totally offensive to her, the partnership deal might help lighten the insult.

He just wished she would say something one way or the other. It wasn't like her to equivocate so much.

Finally she looked up and squinted at him. "What did you just say?"

He smiled. "I'm offering you an associate partnership in our corporation."

Ellie was pretty sure most of the blood in her head had flowed right out, leaving her brain empty and her ears ringing. She felt dizzy and faint and was still not sure she'd understood him. "Say that again, please."

"Partnership, Ellie," he said. "You heard me. I know you want it."

Of course she wanted it. She had brought up the subject of partnership during her review last December, asking the brothers if they had considered adding a partnership track to incentivize their top senior-level employees. Aidan and Logan had admitted they hadn't yet decided, unsure whether they wanted to include anyone else in their tightly knit two-man operation.

"You—you're offering me a partnership position."

"Yes."

"Why?"

"Because you deserve it. And because I'm determined to do whatever it takes to keep you here working with us."

She would've stayed without the partnership offer, but now she was overwhelmed. First he'd offered his own sperm—and everything that went with it, so to speak. Now he was offering her a partnership deal? Had she won the lottery? What was going on?

"Well, what do you think?" he asked.

"I'm stunned," she admitted. "And a little suspicious of the timing of your offer."

He nodded. "I understand how you might feel that way, but the truth is, Logan and I had already planned to make you the offer once he was back from his honeymoon. I'm just speeding up the process." Standing, he walked over and sat down in the chair next to her. He took hold of her hand, warming her all the way through to her heart. "I know you want to have a baby and I want to help you if you'll let me. It's your choice, absolutely, and no matter what you decide, you'll still be a partner and a friend. I brought up the idea with the best of intentions, no matter how idiotic it sounded to you."

"Oh, Aidan."

"Wait." He held up his hand. "I feel honor bound to add that it wouldn't make me uncomfortable at all to see you naked. In fact, it's pretty much all I've thought about lately."

Her throat went dry. Unless she was delusional, it sounded like Aidan was still interested in helping her conceive naturally. And the more she thought about it, the more she was all for it. Especially with him sitting so close and holding her hand and unconsciously rubbing his thumb along the pulse point at her wrist. Tiny zings of excitement charged through her body with every move of his thumb, driving her crazy in all the best ways.

She knew that accepting his offer could be dangerous to her well-being. But it didn't have to be. She was a strong woman and this was essentially a business proposition, after all. It would be the best possible thing for her baby and a fabulous opportunity for her. She could accept without fear of turning into her mother.

Aidan continued, "The partnership deal is my way of letting you know that no matter what you decide on the baby front, we want you to continue working for Sutherland once you've started your family."

"So it's not some sort of bribe to help me forget your good old-fashioned offer?"

"That depends," he said carefully. "Is it working?"

She laughed. "Yes, it's working. I'm weak. But, Aidan,

you don't have to bribe me to stay. I already told you I have every intention of staying on after the baby's born."

"I'm glad. But the partnership is not a bribe. It's for real." He outlined the particulars of the deal, adding that the lawyers would draft an agreement that would take effect immediately upon signing. It was an associate partnership, the first level of the Sutherland partnership track. She had the opportunity to advance each year until she reached the top level of full capital partnership.

"I'll warn you," Aidan said. "Reaching full partnership could take anywhere from five to ten years. But I want to see you go for it."

Go for it, she repeated silently. But could she say yes to the whole deal? she wondered. It might be smart to back away from having a baby with him. After all, if she did agree, it would mean entering into a deeply personal relationship with Aidan that she wasn't sure she would ever recover from.

Still, part of her wanted to shout, *Yes! Yes!* But she was pretty sure those were her hormones talking. She needed to step back and think this through very carefully. Without Aidan around to tempt her.

She mentally collected herself and said, "I need a few days to think about everything you've offered me."

"Everything?" he repeated.

She bit her lip and nodded. "Yes, everything."

He nodded. "All right. I'm leaving for California tomorrow. Why don't you let me know your decision when I get back on Monday."

She gazed at him solemnly. "I'll have an answer for you then."

Three

"We're cleared for takeoff, Mr. Sutherland."

"Thanks, Leslie," Aidan said, and buckled his seat belt.

The flight attendant walked toward the front of the plane to take her own seat behind the partition that separated the passenger compartment from the crew's quarters. Checking his wristwatch, Aidan realized he had six long hours to kill before they would land in California. He made himself comfortable in the sleek leather chair and stretched his long legs out.

As the powerful Gulfstream engines began to roar and the jet took its place in the middle of the runway, it occurred to Aidan that he should've asked Ellie to come along on the trip. At least he'd have someone to talk to during the long flight. It didn't hurt that she was beautiful to look at, too.

She was also smart. And funny. They always laughed a lot when they traveled together. And if she were here, Aidan wouldn't have to wait four days to make love with her.

But since he was forced to wait, he had nothing but time to consider all the potential problems involved with walking into fatherhood. There were plenty. He had never planned on taking this path, but the bottom line was, this was for Ellie and the child who would know both of his parents.

And it meant he could finally have Ellie naked in his bed.

Since she wasn't there, he opened his briefcase and got to work on several of the projects he'd neglected lately. By the time they were flying over California hours later, he was almost caught up on everything.

He looked up as the flight attendant walked into the passenger area. "Guess it's time to buckle up. I can feel the plane starting to descend."

"Yes," Leslie said. "We should be landing in about fifteen minutes."

"Thanks."

Ellie always spent a few hours each weekend in her office, catching up on business journals and studying the stock market. She enjoyed learning new things. Reading articles about business trends and developments helped expand her mind and broaden her horizons and made her better at her job.

Her girlfriends thought she was crazy. Serena urged her not to read the whole weekend away and told her that if she changed her mind, a few of them were meeting in the bar for cocktails and dinner tonight. Ellie wasn't sure she wanted to go out. She had too much to think about.

But that was the problem. With Aidan's proposition still fresh in her mind, she couldn't concentrate on anything else, especially business. Her brain kept bouncing from one idea to the next to…Aidan.

She finally gave up, pushed the books aside and left the office. As she strolled through the lush coco palm grove to the cozy cottage she called home, located on the edge of the resort grounds, she decided the only way she was going to be able to truly relax was to go swimming.

She slipped on her bathing suit, threw on a short cover-up, grabbed a towel and walked down to the beach. The numerous pools scattered around the resort were beautiful, but they were much too lively for relaxation. Ellie preferred to swim in the calm waters of the bay.

The sun was nearing the horizon, but the air was still warm. She touched the clear water with her toe and found it was the perfect temperature, refreshing without giving her a chill. Dropping the towel on the sand, she walked straight into the bay until the water reached her shoulders. Then she plunged her entire body under the water and swam underwater for as long as her breath lasted. Surfacing, she began to swim with slow, easy strokes that stretched her muscles in all the right places.

Ellie had always loved the water. Once upon a time, she had been an excellent swimmer and had even daydreamed of swimming in the Olympic Games. But then her mother died and swimming became a luxury she couldn't afford.

Ellie and Brenna were the only people besides the mortuary director who had attended their mother's funeral. That was when it hit the two girls that they were completely on their own. Their father had no interest in taking custody of them and their mother had no other living relatives. Ellie was thirteen and scared to death to go into foster care, so sixteen-year-old Brenna decided she would do whatever it took to keep them living together in their mother's small house in the same working-class neighborhood where they'd always lived.

Brenna had an after-school job that brought in a few hundred dollars every month. Their eccentric mother had always kept a large stash of money—almost seven thousand dollars—in a safe place in her closet. They lived frugally, only spending money for food and the barest essentials, and managed to stay under the radar for almost four years, until Ellie's junior year in high school. That's when a school counselor grew suspicious of her living situation and contacted the authorities.

Terrified of what might happen next, the girls packed their mother's car with whatever they could grab and in the middle of the night and drove out of town. They headed south and stopped when they reached the outskirts of Atlanta.

For the next eight months, they lived off the grid, sleeping in their car when they couldn't find an available shelter. Brenna took day jobs cleaning houses and Ellie spent hours in the local library studying for her GED.

They'd survived, Ellie thought as she swam through the balmy water. More than that, they'd thrived, depending on each other and building a bond stronger than most sisters could claim.

A few hundred yards from shore, she stopped, treaded water and stared up at the vivid streaks of orange, pink and purple that filled the sky as the sun sank into the sea.

Looking back at the resort, she still couldn't quite believe that this was her life. She'd come a long way from those days of living in a car. Life hadn't exactly been easy-breezy back then, but she and her sister had stayed together and they had endured.

Soon after Ellie obtained her GED, she turned eighteen and they didn't have to worry about the authorities anymore. They'd rented a small apartment, Ellie had enrolled at the local college and Brenna had started her own housecleaning service.

As she turned and paddled back to shore, Ellie continued to dwell on the strange path her life had taken. She had missed out on so much during those years. Childhood friendships, boys, shopping, cute clothes, the prom, sporting events—all the fun things that normal teenage girls did.

But it couldn't be helped. She and Brenna had realized early on that they couldn't afford to stand out, couldn't afford to have anyone examine their lives too closely.

So there would be no boyfriends, no close girlfriends, no activities that might draw attention. Instead, Ellie had escaped into books, newspapers, magazines, blotting out the hard times while soaking up every morsel of information she could get. And once she got into college, it was as if she was making up for all the time she'd lost in her last year of high school. She'd made some nice girlfriends and even dated once in a while. But more than anything else, she studied constantly, couldn't learn fast enough. Her so-called photographic memory, along with a near fanatical need to succeed, helped her graduate in three years. She had been so captivated by the inner workings of corporations that she had already obtained her MBA when most of her peers were wondering what to wear to the homecoming game.

Now she was happily employed by the Sutherland Corporation, where she was considered brilliant, independent and overachieving—in a good way. She had great friends and she'd dated a few men. She had the means and opportunity to have a child and give that child everything she hadn't had while growing up.

She reached the beach, grabbed her towel and patted it against her wet skin. The sand was still warm on her feet although the sun had set long minutes ago.

"That's enough reminiscing," she muttered aloud as she brushed the water off her arms and legs.

Why had she dredged up all those ancient memories? She rarely thought of the old days anymore. Did they have something to do with Brenna's ultrasound picture? Or were they somehow connected to Aidan's proposition? Were the memories a reminder of how tired she was of always missing out on all the fun?

Because it suddenly dawned on her that if she said yes to Aidan, she wouldn't only be doing it to get herself pregnant. No, she would also be doing it because sex with Aidan would be exciting and *fun*.

And after all these years, Ellie deserved to have some fun. Didn't she?

And speaking of fun, she thought as she grabbed her towel off the sand, her girlfriends would be in the bar at seven o'clock. With a determination she hadn't felt in a while, she wrapped the towel around her waist and walked briskly toward home. If she took a speedy shower and dressed quickly, she could meet the girls in time to buy the first round of drinks.

Aidan never saw the sneak attack coming. In retrospect, he figured that's why they called it a *sneak* attack.

It was two days into his California visit and his cousin Cameron Duke was throwing a pool party in the backyard of his home overlooking Dunsmuir Bay. Aidan lazed on a comfy raft in Cameron's pool, a cold beer perched in the handy bottle holder. The cacophony of kids screaming joyfully, a dog barking, Sally taking orders for sangria, all faded into the background as Aidan tried to remember how long it had been since he'd been able to relax like this. Six months? Longer? Hell, the corporation had been in high gear and he'd been working nonstop for the last year at least.

The sun was warm, the water cool, and as the noise level began to die down, Aidan wished again that he'd brought Ellie with him to California. She would've enjoyed herself and fit right in with this lively crowd. But more than that, he wanted her with him right now, here in the pool, her body wet and slick against his....

Suddenly without warning, the air was filled with screeching banshees as a giant gush of water exploded all around him. Seconds later, more water engulfed him as kids and grownups cannonballed into the pool from every angle.

"Hey!" He scrambled off the raft, grabbing the beer bottle as pool water surged from one end to the other, splashing the deck and creating a mini-tsunami.

"Good save," Brandon shouted above the uproar of the skirmish. "Never waste a perfectly good beer."

Aidan laughed. "My philosophy exactly."

Brandon was the biggest of the three Duke brothers, a former star quarterback in the NFL. Sitting on his broad shoulders was Samantha, his brother Cameron's adorable, curly-haired three-year-old. She laughed and splashed and occasionally smacked the top of Brandon's head like a conga drum.

Abruptly, little hands latched on to Aidan's shoulders. He turned and found Jake, Cameron's five-year-old son, grinning maniacally at him.

"Piggyback ride!" the little boy cried.

"Uh." Aidan looked around to see if there was a parent nearby. The pool was filled with them, but they were all busy with the other kids. Damn. Aidan was on his own.

"Okay, kiddo," Aidan said. "Guess you're stuck with me."

Jake didn't seem to mind. "Go! Go!"

"Okay, okay," Aidan muttered. "Hold on tight," he warned as the boy climbed onto his back. Then Aidan glanced around for somewhere to put the beer bottle he'd saved only moments before, setting it down safely on the flat tile surface that surrounded the pool.

He took off slowly and jogged around the pool, being careful to keep Jake's head above the water line. Looking around, though, he wasn't sure it mattered. All these Duke kids swam like fish, even the youngest ones.

After a few minutes, Aidan glanced back. "Had enough?"

"Nope," Jake said, slapping Aidan's back. "More."

A half hour later, Aidan came to a stop on the shallow-end steps. "I'm worn out, kiddo."

"Okay, you better rest," Jake said. The little boy wrapped his arms around Aidan's neck and hugged him, pressing his cheek to Aidan's. "Thanks, Uncle Aidan." Then he hopped off and swam away.

Aidan swam to the side of the pool and grabbed his beer, refusing to admit how much he had enjoyed the squirmy little kid hanging around his neck.

Three hours later, after Aidan had eaten his body weight in grilled burgers, the best potato salad he'd ever had and Sally's cherry cobbler, he glanced around the spacious patio. The grownups were still gathered at the table talking while the little kids fought mightily to stay awake, but failed miserably.

Five-year-old Jake, the oldest of the kids, had decided to take a trip down the jungle gym slide and had promptly tossed his cookies. Without batting an eye, Cameron rushed him into the house to clean him up.

For some reason, all the efficient family activity reminded Aidan of Ellie and her ability to keep things running smoothly under any circumstance. Of course, everything lately reminded him of the woman waiting for him back home on Alleria. He couldn't wait to go home and get her naked. There wasn't a question in his mind but that she would want the same thing.

A few minutes later, Jake came running outside in fresh pajamas and shocked the hell out of Aidan by climbing onto his lap. Now the little guy was sound asleep in his arms. Talk about a sneak attack. Aidan couldn't quite fathom how all these protective feelings for this scrawny little guy had cropped up.

Was this the kind of emotional stuff that dads went

through? he wondered. Was this what he'd signed on for with Ellie? No, he realized quickly. If Ellie said yes to his offer tomorrow, Aidan would one day become a dad in name only. He would be there for financial support and the occasional family gathering. He rubbed his chest absently, relieved that he wouldn't have to deal with these overwhelming feelings of fear and concern and love and—

"Here you go." Cameron handed him a heavy crystal glass of single malt scotch. "Don't worry about waking up Jake. I swear that kid can sleep through earthquakes and enemy fire."

Cameron sat and both men sipped their drinks in companionable silence, watching the activity around them.

"Time for jammies," Brandon's wife Kelly announced, and scooped tiny Robbie up off the lawn, where he'd been speed crawling, trying to make his escape. The kid put up a halfhearted fuss but after a moment, he laid his head on Kelly's shoulder and closed his eyes.

"This one's zonked out, too," Adam said, and carried T.J. into the house. His wife Trish was already inside taking care of the latest addition to their family, two-month-old Annabelle.

Cameron shook his head. "Never thought the day would come when there'd be more kids than adults at a Duke brothers party."

"The kids are great," Aidan said, and took a sip of scotch.

Cameron laughed. "Spoken like a die-hard bachelor determined never to have any of his own."

"Hey, I meant it," Aidan protested, then shrugged sheepishly. "Is it that obvious?"

"I recognize the code words." Cameron relaxed in his chair. "Kids are great as long as they're someone else's, right?"

Aidan chuckled. He might've been guilty of uttering

those very words on more than one occasion. Oddly enough though, tonight he had liked the feel of Jake, trusting and sound asleep, tucked up against him. Wow. He couldn't believe he'd just had that thought.

"I was never gonna have any of my own, either," Cameron said. "None of us were. Hell, my brothers and I made a sacred pact when we were young. No marriage. No kids. Ever."

Aidan frowned at the familiar sentiment. "So what happened?"

"Julia happened," he said simply. "And Jake. Mom had something to say about it. Come to think of it, my brothers added their two cents' worth, too."

"Sounds like a united front. What'd they all say to change your mind?"

Just then, Julia stood and eased little Jake off of Aidan's lap and into her arms. "I'll take him in to bed."

Cameron jumped up. "Let me do it."

"No, you stay and talk to Aidan," she said, and reached up and kissed him before walking away.

Aidan took another sip of scotch and wondered how quickly he could leave to get home to Ellie.

At fifty thousand feet, Aidan stared out the window at the cloud cover below. He and his father and taken care of their family business so Aidan had left a day early, anxious to get back to the island. So far, he'd spent most of the flight reminiscing about the last few days with his father and Sally and the rest of the Dukes. It was still a little weird to realize that he and his dad and brother were suddenly part of a great big loving family they'd never known until two years ago.

And he wondered what it said about him that he could still feel the imprint of little Jake's slippery wet fingers clinging to his shoulders in the pool. The kid had gotten to him, along with the rest of the brood.

Who'd have guessed that he and Logan would end up with a loud, active extended family after all these years? Growing up, it had been the three of them alone: Aidan, his brother and their dad. But now things were changing. Their family was changing and growing. Was that change another reason why he'd made up his mind so easily about offering to father Ellie's child? He wasn't prepared to answer that just yet.

To divert himself, he stared out the windows. The cloud cover had dissipated and he tried to guess what area of the country they were flying over.

"Looks like Louisiana," he murmured, gazing down at the verdant surface a mile below. Rivulets intertwined like snakes through miles of lush growth and trees, emptying into small lakes and ponds. Bayou, he thought. Definitely Louisiana. That meant he had another two hours in the air before they reached Alleria.

He leaned both arms on the high back of the leather seat and thought of his own unhappy youth. His mother had walked out on the family when he and his brother were seven years old. Both Aidan and Logan always vowed to stay single because women couldn't be trusted. Their mother wasn't the only woman in the world who'd proven that theory true.

And after hearing his cousin Cameron's story about what he'd been through with his own miserable father, it just went to show that there were plenty of men who couldn't be trusted either.

Hell, Aidan knew that. But it hadn't hit so close to home before. Cameron Duke's old man was a son of a bitch.

Aidan realized that he and Logan had really lucked out in that realm. Their father Tom was the best dad any kid could ever have.

But their mother was a mess. Not that she had ever beaten them, or starved or lashed out at them. No, his mother's sins were ones of neglect and abandonment. She just didn't care.

She'd never even taken the trouble to figure out which of them was Aidan and which was Logan. She used to look at one brother or the other and say, "Which one are you?"

That was pathetic, but it wasn't criminal.

So yes, their dad was the best there ever was. But Aidan still had his mother's genes. He'd always worried that he might turn out like his mom and be a terrible parent who only cared about his own selfish needs. But it didn't have to be that way, he realized now. He knew himself, knew he would never be like her. By making his offer to Ellie, he knew her child would be in good hands. Ellie would make a wonderful mother and Aidan would be there to support them both.

Aidan shook away all thoughts of his mother and focused instead on his dad. It had been so good to see him interacting with Sally and all the Dukes, almost as if they'd always been a family. They had welcomed all three Sutherland men unconditionally, but Aidan got a special kick from seeing his dad so happy.

"I have your lunch ready for you, Mr. Sutherland," Leslie said.

"Thanks." Beyond grateful for the distraction, Aidan put aside all those thoughts and sat to wolf down the perfectly cooked pasta and salmon Leslie had prepared. While he ate, he flipped through a business magazine and made some notes. Afterward, he put the finishing touches on some contracts he'd brought with him, then slid his briefcase away for the rest of the flight.

Aidan poured himself a glass of wine and tried to relax. The plane was over the Gulf of Mexico and he couldn't wait to get home. He was getting more and more anxious to see Ellie again and he'd convinced himself that she'd made her decision to take him up on his plan.

He almost laughed when he thought about how he'd planned to find a woman while he was in California. Who knew his feelings would change so drastically in a week? Now all he could think about was Ellie. He couldn't wait to see her again.

He recalled her nervousness about "getting naked" with him and chuckled, thinking he could hardly wait to calm her nerves.

Unbidden, an image of little Jake popped into his head. Weird, wasn't it? Aidan was a man who had never wanted children and yet he was willing to father a child for his business associate. He squirmed a little uneasily in his seat. Fathering a child and *being* a father were two different things though, he assured himself. The baby would be his blood and would have his full support throughout his life. That didn't mean he would be interacting with it on a daily basis.

And at that thought, another memory of Jake, curled up and asleep on his lap, zipped through Aidan's mind. He scowled and pushed it out again. He wasn't interested in being anyone's dad. But he was most definitely interested in Ellie and in making sure she had the best for the little family she wanted to create.

Of course, on the off chance that she was still feeling ambivalent, he would be happy to make the decision for her. The thought of getting her naked had become a bit of an obsession with him, so if she needed persuading, he was the man to do it.

He sat back in his seat and smiled at the different ways he'd be willing to use to convince Ellie to agree to his offer.

"I've got to go inside," Ellie said, sitting up on her beach towel and stretching like a sleepy cat. She'd been daydreaming for the last hour about Aidan. Oh, who was she kidding? She'd been thinking about him all weekend, wondering what it would be like to have sex with him. She would find out soon enough and the thought made her equally nervous and thrilled. He would be back tomorrow and she couldn't wait to see him again.

But she had to make sure their arrangement remained strictly business. Yes, she would enjoy herself with Aidan, but she would never allow herself to slide into a state of pure unadulterated passion from which she might never recover. The danger was self-evident; she was, after all, her mother's daughter.

So to maintain the business aspect of the deal, Ellie had spent all day yesterday preparing a computerized list of objectives, rules and contingencies. Once Aidan was back in the office, she would present it to him and explain everything in detail so that they were both on the same page going forward.

She spent a long moment adjusting her eyes to the sun, then stood and began to gather her things.

"Are you sure?" Serena asked, not moving an inch from her beach towel. "It feels so good to lay here and do nothing."

"That's all I've done today," Ellie lamented, as she tossed her sunblock and paperback novel into her small carryall. "I've become a slug."

"I'm so proud of you." Serena sat up and used her hand to block the sun from her eyes. "And I love that new bikini of yours."

"The one you forced me to buy?" Ellie laughed.

"Yes, and you're welcome," Serena said. "It looks fantastic on you."

Ellie felt positively decadent after four hours of doing nothing but swimming and sunning on the small patch of beachfront at the far end of the resort area. Few guests ever ventured down this way so the Alleria employees were welcome to sunbathe here. It was the first time Ellie had ever taken advantage of that perk; the change was thanks to Serena.

Also, thanks to Serena, she'd spent way too much money on a flattering two-piece bathing suit they'd found in one of the resort's fancy shops. That was after Serena had taken one look at Ellie's serviceable one-piece tank suit and been horrified.

"You're a bad influence on me," Ellie said as she reached for her towel and shook the sand off.

"My work here is done." Serena sighed and stood up. "Guess I'd better get going, too. I need to prep a few things for my staff meeting tomorrow morning."

Ellie left Serena at her house and kept walking until she reached her own cottage another few hundred yards away. Her feet were gritty from the sand and her skin was drenched in sunblock, so before going inside, she stopped to use the outdoor shower near the kitchen door.

She tossed her cover-up onto the veranda and stepped under the stream of cool water. She savored the feeling as it splashed against her warm skin, trying to imagine how it would be if Aidan were showering with her. Wonderful, she thought, and slowly ran her hands along her arms and legs and stomach to brush off the sand.

Aidan dropped off his bag and briefcase in his suite, then jogged over to the business offices to find Ellie. She always spent Sunday afternoons at her desk, catching up on business news and any loose ends that needed to be nipped before the work week started.

She wouldn't be expecting him a day early and he figured he'd be catching her off guard. He wondered if he would be able to tell by the look on her face whether or not she was willing to get naked with him—as she put it. Or would they have to discuss things further? Somehow he knew she'd made up her mind. Ellie rarely hesitated when it came to decision making, although, granted, this situation was a unique one.

He strolled past her secretary's desk and went straight to her office door. It was closed so he knocked, then immediately opened it and walked in. "Ellie, I'm back. Did you have a chance to…"

She wasn't at her desk.

Okay, not a big surprise. It was Sunday afternoon, after all. So maybe she was doing laundry or cleaning her house. He crossed the busy lobby and headed outside, taking a shortcut through the main pool area and past the tiki bar. The din of music and laughter faded as he made his way across the property to the residence cottages on the other side of the coco palm garden.

As he neared Ellie's house, he heard a woman singing. One of her neighbors, no doubt. Not a bad voice, he thought, although it sounded a little garbled, like the singer was under water.

None of their guests ever stayed over here in the residence cottages, so it had to be an employee. At least it wasn't Ellie, Aidan knew that much. His prim, proper, straight-laced senior vice president would never…

He stopped in his tracks as he caught sight of the dazzling backside of a woman standing under an outdoor shower, wearing what could charitably be called a string bikini.

His mind shut down as raw primordial need took over. Words formed in his brain, but he couldn't utter them aloud. Sexy. Gorgeous. Body. Want. Now.

Mine.

The woman continued singing, completely oblivious to Aidan's presence. As his mind slowly clicked back into working order, the term *poleaxed* came to mind. He was pretty sure this was what it felt like to be smacked over the head with a two-by-four. He'd never seen anything so stunning in his life.

As the woman rubbed her hands over her skin, Aidan had to bite his tongue to keep from offering to do it for her. Finally she reached for the spigot, cut off the water and turned.

And Aidan felt his chin hit the ground.

Ellie?

Four

Aidan had never seen his senior vice president in a bathing suit before, let alone something like the teasingly skimpy scraps of material she was wearing now. Hard to believe, but the real Ellie was even better than the sexy dream images that had been invading his mind the whole time he was away.

Okay, he thought. *Yeah. He could definitely do this.*

Ellie's eyes were still closed as she wiped water off her face and smoothed her hair back.

Aidan couldn't speak, could only gawk like some teenager at her awe-inspiring breasts. They were barely covered by the jungle-print scraps of material, but they were high and round and perfect for him. Perfect for his hands. Perfect for his mouth.

Her stomach was smooth and touchable, her hips round and shapely and delicious, and her legs…had he already mentioned touchable? What about delicious?

"Ellie?"

Her eyes popped open and she let out a squeal. "Aidan?"

He kind of wished he hadn't said anything as she slung one arm across her breasts. With her other hand, she tried to cover the enchanting apex of her thighs.

"What're you doing here?" she cried. "Oh, no! This is… Oh, just…let me get dressed!"

"Not necessary," he insisted, but she was already running up the steps to her front door. "It's just a bathing suit. I've seen them before."

"Not on me!" She fumbled with her keys and dropped them. "It's unprofessional."

True, Aidan thought. He had to give her that one. Seeing her like this wiped away every image he had of her prim, proper business attire.

"Ellie, stop worrying about it. It's the weekend. You're not at work."

She continued to protest. But suddenly his ears were no longer capable of hearing as she bent over to retrieve her keys, giving him a stunning view of her world-class derriere.

Oh, dear lord. He could die a happy man now.

"You weren't supposed to be home until tomorrow," she said. "I'm…surprised, that's all. Let me take this off. I mean, change into something more suitable."

"Ellie." He snatched the keys from her hand, jammed the proper one into the lock and pushed the door open for her. "We live and work on an island. A *tropical* island. A resort. Everyone wears bathing suits around here—" Though not as well as she did, he added silently. "Quit making such a big deal about this. I don't care."

"I know," she muttered, "but I'm not used to you seeing me—to me being dressed like—to have you show up at my house and—" She blew out a breath and took another one. "Never mind. Well. You're home early."

"Yeah," he said, gazing down at her. "Hi."

"Hi," she whispered.

She was so close, he could almost taste her. Lust had him reaching to pull her closer. As her breasts skimmed his chest, she gulped and pushed away.

"I'm all wet," she said, her voice raspy.

"Again, let me say I don't care," he said.

"I do."

Her voice gave her away and he knew she was affected by the moment. But apparently she was going to fight it. She brushed past him and stepped inside, then waved him in after her.

"You wait here," she said. "I'll just be a minute."

Aidan acceded to her wishes even though he wanted to follow her right into her bedroom and have his way with her, but that would be pushing it. Right?

Frowning, he watched her scurry from the room; then, alone, he took a moment to look around. He'd never been inside Ellie's cottage before, he realized. Restless, he wandered the room, picking out the touches that Ellie had added to make it her own.

Aidan and Logan had chosen the California Craftsman style for these two-bedroom residential cottages. Inside, the designers had added Caribbean flair to the traditional sturdiness with pale painted walls, blond wood floors, ceiling fans, lots of windows and vivid island fabrics on the furniture. Those details gave the rooms more charm and lightness than what was usually found in corporate housing.

But this cottage carried the stamp of Ellie's personality. There were surprising bits and pieces of her personal style everywhere he looked. Colorful pillows were scattered across the couch and chairs. A set of watercolor paintings showed striped umbrellas on the beach and children playing at water's edge. A whimsical bowl of papier-mâché fruit was the centerpiece on the small dining room table. And on every shelf there were framed photographs of friends or relatives, plus knickknacks, seashells, a small bowl of dried leaves and twigs. And books. Lots of books.

"I'm sorry to keep you waiting," she said, rushing back into the room.

"It's not a job interview, Ellie."

"No, of course not." She wore pale linen pants and a thin, sleeveless red blouse. Her hair was still wet but combed and tucked behind her ears. Her feet were bare. She looked almost as delectable right now as she had in her bikini a few minutes ago.

Why hadn't he noticed how sexy and beautiful she was the minute he'd hired her? He'd worked with her for four years and the thought had never crossed his mind until recently. Maybe he needed more than an eye exam. Maybe the doctors should take a look at his brain.

She straightened a magazine on the end table. "So, have you been back long? Would you like something to drink? Did you have a nice weekend with your family?"

She was still nervous. He had to admit he liked it. It was good to know he wasn't the only one affected by that sizzling moment or two they had shared on the front porch. But as tight and uncomfortable as his body was feeling right at the moment, Aidan had to smile. Surely Ellie was the only woman in the world who would expect a man to indulge in small talk so soon after—

After what?

Nothing had happened, really. Nothing like what he wanted to happen anyway.

"Aidan?" She was watching him. "Did you hear me?"

Over the roaring in his blood? Just barely. But he answered her questions anyway.

"I did. I've been home an hour. No, thank you, I don't want a drink. And yes, seeing the family was great," he answered in order of the questions she asked. Casually leaning one shoulder against the heavy bookshelf, he said, "Look, I know I'm home a day early, but I couldn't wait to see you. You know why I'm here, right? I'm hoping you have an answer for me. Do you, Ellie?"

"Um, yes. About that." She fiddled with one of her shirt buttons fretfully, causing him to fixate on her breasts even more than before. She seemed to realize what she was doing because she dropped her hands abruptly and gazed up at him. "I would prefer to discuss it tomorrow in the office."

"You want to discuss it in the office," he repeated slowly as he gave her a cool, assessing look. "Because it's…business?"

"Well, no, but yes." She frowned, annoyed at herself. After taking a deep breath and letting it out slowly, she continued. "Yes, Aidan. It is business. Anything that involves relations between you and me will have an effect on our business dealings. And after all, we'll be signing both a contract and a partnership agreement. Our lives and our jobs are about to become inextricably intertwined, wouldn't you agree?"

Damn, Aidan thought. Even when she got all prim and proper on him, he wanted her. Badly. Now that he'd given himself permission to want her, he couldn't seem to stop.

"Now, you made me a proposition," she continued, "and I would like to negotiate the terms. In that regard, I went ahead and made a list of conditions along with some facts and figures I'd like to go over with you. Tomorrow. In the office."

She'd made a list. Why was he not surprised? But he was impressed and gave her high marks for presenting her case so eloquently. So why did he just want to grab her and kiss her? He would, he vowed. And soon. But right now, it was obvious that Ellie needed to exert some control over the situation, so he was happy to allow it. For now. "Let me first get one thing straight, Ellie. The bottom line is, your answer is yes. You've decided to go ahead with my plan."

"Well, yes. But my conditions—"

"Are on a list," he drawled. "At the office."

"Yes," she said primly. "That's right."

He spied her tablet computer, the one she carried with her at all times, on the side table next to her purse and briefcase. "Do you have a copy of the list on your tablet?"

"Yes, but it's not as effective at making a presentation as my—"

"Let's see it."

"But—"

"Ellie." He pushed away from the bookshelf and approached her. "I don't mind sitting through your *presentation* tomorrow, pie charts, Venn diagrams and all. But I'd like the main issues settled right here, right now."

She scowled, but appeared ready to concede. A good thing since he considered it a very reasonable request.

"Fine." She grabbed her tablet, started it up, then scrolled through several pages to get to her list.

"Wait, let me see that." He turned the tablet so he could view the screen and laughed. "Roman numerals? Bullet points? This isn't a list, it's a business presentation. That's why you wanted to go over it at the office. You created a slide show for me."

Her eyes narrowed and her voice went cold and tight. "I happen to think better with bullet points." She folded her arms tightly across her chest. "Stop laughing."

But she was biting back a smile, so Aidan knew she wasn't too deeply offended. He was just glad she didn't have any clue how badly his body parts were throbbing at the sight of her lush breasts straining against the thin material of her blouse. She might change her attitude.

He ripped his gaze away from her and stared at the

screen. She had divided her list into several main topics: Pre-pregnancy and pregnancy. Post-pregnancy. Baby care and support issues.

Okay, she got points for taking an organized approach to life, but talk about a buzzkill. Time to take back control of this situation. "Send me the pertinent points and I'll have the lawyers draft the agreement we talked about."

"I'll do that," she said. "But that's all about the future. I would like to go over the current issues that concern you and me."

"You and me?" he said, wondering why he'd thought this would be easy. A woman with a sharp, intelligent brain could be a dangerous thing, he reminded himself. "What about you and me? You already said you agreed to my idea."

"Oh, I do agree," she rushed to say. "I thought it all through and I'm very happy to go ahead with the plan. I'm certain that your sperm will be suitable."

"Suitable? Damn, Ellie." He chuckled as he pulled her close to him, but she stopped him again.

"Please, Aidan. You're distracting me and I'd really like you to watch my slide presentation first. It only runs ten minutes and I went to a lot of trouble to make sure everything was covered. I think it'll help clarify our duties and responsibilities to each other."

"Duties and responsibilities?" Aidan shook his head. Leave it to Ellie to explain sex using bullet points.

"Yes," she said. "That's the key to understanding our roles in this project, don't you think?"

"Our *project?*" he said.

"Well, yes. That's how I like to see it. We're collaborating toward achieving a tangible goal and we have guidelines and milestones to meet." She shifted to his side and held up her tablet so they could both get a look at the screen.

"If you'll allow me to go through my slide presentation, all will be explained."

He placed his hands on her shoulders in a sincere gesture. "I admire and respect you, Ellie, but I'm not going to sit through a long slide presentation that explains how to have sex."

"Oh, but this isn't about the *how*. It's more about the *why* and the *when* and the...well, if I can proceed?"

"Fine," he said, gritting his teeth. First time for everything, he told himself. And if it meant having her in his bed, he would force himself to listen. "Let her rip."

"Thank you. Now it's—"

"But I think you're stalling," he said, turning to her. "Believe me, I know my duties and responsibilities. I know how to deliver my extremely healthy sperm the old-fashioned way. And I think we're both in agreement on what we want, right? So I'd say we're ready to get started." He brushed his knuckles slowly down her arm.

She swallowed carefully. "Ready. Oh, yes. Um." She shook her hair back and seemed to regroup. Gripping the tablet again, she said brightly, "That's all covered in item six. Let's just go over the others."

Before he could argue further, she slid her finger across the surface to reveal the first slide. Aidan's eyes were inexorably drawn to the screen. Damned if she hadn't come up with a full-bore bullet point agenda covering his duties and responsibilities, right down to his diet preferences and clothing choices. Some experts thought that the correct choices in both areas were essential toward making his sperm more motile.

The woman's responsibilities were just as eye-opening. There were estrogen hormone levels to be tested and she would have to monitor her temperature. And then there was something called the luteal phase, which caused a little chill to run up his spine. The very word sounded vaguely sinister.

It was all strangely mesmerizing, like a traffic accident on a California freeway. Gruesome and shocking, but he couldn't look away.

The last page was a month-by-month production schedule. Ellie gave him a moment to review it, then said, "I don't have my calendar with me, but luckily, I've already memorized the days."

"Luckily," he muttered, then decided he'd waited long enough. She continued to speak as he leaned in and kissed her neck.

She gasped, then moaned. He moved his lips to her earlobe, then down to her shoulder. After a long moment, she tried to continue. "I'm s-scheduled to start ovulating in the next five to seven d-days, so if you can arrange your schedule, we should have s-sex beginning Friday night and… and…oh, my…continuing through the following Wednesday night, with S-Sunday and Monday being the most optimum days."

He took the tablet and set it down on the table. He'd seen enough. More than enough. Talk about information overload. His eyes were bleeding.

He appreciated that Ellie was ultra-organized, but it was time to lighten things up, even if it meant throwing a wrench or two into her well-ordered plans.

"Only at night?" he wondered, as he urged her closer and ran his hands slowly along her spine, down to her supple bottom. "What about the mornings?"

"Mornings?" she said on a soft sigh. "What do you mean?"

"Some would argue it's the best time of the day for what you have in mind."

"Oh, but—"

"Or lunchtime," he said, leaning back to stare into her eyes. "Sex in the office might be fun, Ellie. We can use my conference table."

"Now you're teasing me."

"You think so?" he said. Her expression was so vulnerable, so earnest, that he wanted to ease her into bed—or onto the dining room table—right here and now. In fact, that was a damn good idea.

"Aidan, I don't think you're listening. This is important."

"I'm listening," he assured her as he slipped his arm around her shoulders and walked her over to the couch, where he urged her to sit down with him. "But for now, let's skip to the bottom line. I'll help you get pregnant and I'll help provide for your child. You'll have a partnership with Sutherland Corp. and stay here on Alleria. We'll have contracts drawn up that specify all the points you've talked about."

"Well, yes, but there's more to discuss."

"The thing is, Ellie, I don't think we should be too rigid about this. After all, we don't want to put too much pressure on you."

"Pressure?" she said, then frowned. "Do you think I'm being rigid? Be honest."

"Of course not," he said, absently skimming his thumb along the soft skin of her arm. "It's smart to cover all the bases."

"Thanks. I think so, too, and I'm glad you agree."

"Good. But as long as we're covering bases, I think waiting until Friday is problematic. It would be better to get started right away."

She considered that little bombshell. "But it won't be any use if the timing isn't right."

"But think about it, Ellie," he said. "You're going to be nervous all the way from now until next Friday night, and that's never a good thing. It'll take a lot of pressure off you if we started practicing right away." Damn, that was a good one, Aidan thought to himself. "That way, next week when the timing is critical, we'll know what we're doing. We'll be ahead of the game."

She stared up at him. "Something tells me you already know what you're doing."

"I do," he said helpfully. "But I'm not the one we're concerned about. You are. And there's something else you might not have considered."

Frowning, she said, "What's that?"

"You probably ought to decide what kind of sex you'd like to have the first time. Plenty of experts say that that's the key to assuring that the entire…*project* goes well."

Her eyes narrowed with doubt. "Why does that matter?"

"It goes a long way toward dispelling the nervousness factor," he explained.

She bit her lip. "I'm afraid I don't have a lot of experience in differentiating the types."

"I do." He turned on the couch to face her so he could see her reactions. "I'll name off a few and you can decide where you'd like to start. There's funny sex, of course. Lots of laughs, no pressure, very relaxing. And there's romantic sex. You know, a little champagne, roses, soft jazz in the background."

"Oh, I like that," she whispered.

"Yeah, that's a crowd pleaser," he said, warming up to his subject. "And then you've got your naughty sex."

She swallowed carefully. "I'm not sure about that one."

"We'll try it out so you can be sure though, right?"

"Um…"

"There are plenty of other choices, too," he continued nonchalantly. "And once you've decided on a type, there are additional factors to consider. Like style, for instance.

Do you want it slow and easy? Fast and hot? Break the glass sex? Swing from the ceiling sex?"

Slowly but surely, the color of her cheeks had turned a deep rose. So he'd managed to excite her a little. He hoped so, hoped she was as turned on by this conversation as he was.

He had to discreetly adjust himself as she licked her lips. "Some of those sound complicated. And dangerous."

"I'll make sure we're perfectly safe." He took her hand in his. "Look, why don't you let me be in charge of those decisions. At least in the beginning."

She let out a sigh of relief. "I would appreciate that."

"And we'll start Tuesday night."

"But that's the day after tomorrow."

"Right," he said. "My place. Eight o'clock."

Alarmed, she stared at him. "But that's too soon."

"I don't think so," he said, smoothing a strand of her hair back behind her ear. "In fact, I think we should get a few preliminaries out of the way right now. After all, practice makes perfect."

And with that, he covered her mouth with his in a kiss that she met with such need and all-consuming heat, he wondered if he would survive until Tuesday.

Aidan was right about one thing, Ellie thought on Tuesday, as she struggled to pay attention to her notes on a new contract. She was going to be nervous until the deed was done. Maybe it really was better that they'd decided to start having sex right away. She would hate to feel so jangled up in knots for another full week.

So, yeah, she thought. Good thing she was having sex tonight. With Aidan. At eight o'clock. Tonight. Oh, mercy.

She had almost thought they'd get the whole thing started the other night when he'd come to her house. The way he had looked at her after her shower had almost turned the cool water on her skin to steam. And the way he'd described all those different types of sex? She knew he'd been goading her, but it had worked. And then he'd kissed her. She'd been so wound up, it was a wonder she hadn't jumped him right then and there, on her couch. In bright daylight.

Naughty sex? She exhaled heavily. She'd heard about naughty sex but had never experienced anything close to it. The two measly sexual encounters she'd had in the past could easily be placed at the farthest opposite end of the spectrum from naughty.

The first time had been a fumbling, blind-leading-the-blind failure. The second time wasn't much better. They were both with Teddy, her history study partner in college.

He had seemed like a nice guy in class, so she'd agreed to go out with him a few times. Their dates were pleasant so, even after his bumbling sexual attempts, she would've continued seeing him if she hadn't overheard him bragging to his friends a few days later. Teddy was so sure she would soon be drowning in the afterglow of his awesome lovemaking that he would be able to induce her to do all his homework from then on.

Seriously? Men could be very weird.

On the other hand, Ellie had no doubt that Aidan was an expert in all things naughty. She pictured his tanned hands sliding up her thighs to explore her deepest depths while his clever mouth rained kisses down her neck, along her breasts, across her stomach and farther down her body....

The contract notes were forgotten as she shoved her chair back from her desk and stood. And breathed. It wouldn't do to faint in her office in the middle of the afternoon. But gosh, she was anxious to get this over with. But, she amended, please don't have it be over too fast. He would make it last for a while, wouldn't he? Aidan would do what he could to make it pleasurable for her. Wouldn't he?

"Of course he will, you knucklehead," she muttered aloud. For heaven's sake, he was so sexy, so masculine, so sure of himself, it wouldn't take much effort at all for him to send her zooming straight to heaven.

Besides, none of the women she'd seen him with over the years had ever looked as though they were disappointed in his company. She frowned at that thought. Aidan had been with dozens of women. How was she going to measure up? Her experience was so small it hardly counted. This could be very embarrassing.

"But you're not in a relationship," she told herself. "This is business. Strictly business."

They were only going through with this *project* so that Ellie could get pregnant. Sending her shivering into ecstasy was not a necessary part of the agenda. Pregnancy was. That was the bottom line. And as a businesswoman, she was all about the bottom line.

But she shivered a little anyway, just thinking about Aidan in bed with her. Touching her. Kissing her. Nibbling her.

"Oh, God." She sucked in more deep breaths to calm herself down. Then, glancing back at her desk, she shook her head.

Aidan had been wrapped up in conference calls all day, so Ellie had honestly thought she would get a lot of work done today. But no. She was useless. The contract would have to wait another day. She was going to go home and pamper herself and get ready for her big night. In bed. With Aidan.

Rolling her eyes at her own foolishness, she grabbed her purse and left the office.

The scene was set for romantic sex.

Aidan glanced around the living room of his penthouse suite and approved of what he saw. He had always been a romantic guy and enjoyed the trappings that went along with it. So he felt confident as he instructed his catering guy where to place the ice bucket and the dessert he'd selected for tonight.

If there was one thing Aidan Sutherland knew how to do, it was set the scene for sex. But this time, he had to admit, he was really enjoying himself, picturing Ellie walking in and seeing all this. Candlelight, champagne on ice, chocolate mousse with whipped cream for dessert, soft, sultry jazz playing low in the background, dozens of roses and star lilies arranged in different vases around the suite.

The doorbell rang and he strolled over to open the door. And couldn't help but smile. Her hair was lifted up off her neck with a few wavy tendrils curling down. He'd never seen her wear her hair like that, but it suited her and made him glad he'd decided to dwell on romance tonight. She wore sexy, strappy sandals and was dressed in a short, colorful sarong-style skirt that wrapped around her waist and a thin turquoise top that accentuated her breasts.

That's how Aidan saw it anyhow. Now that he'd seen her in that bikini, he was pretty sure everything she wore from now on would accentuate her breasts.

"You made it," he said, swinging the door wide to let her in.

She smiled. "Did you think I wouldn't?"

He closed the door behind her. "You looked a little preoccupied in the office today. I wondered if you might be having second thoughts."

No," she said with a firm nod. "This is the plan we agreed on and I'm ready to go through with it."

He pursed his lips in a twisted grin. "There's no firing squad in here, Ellie. You can relax. In fact, I've got just the thing to help us both unwind." He led her over to the dining area, where he popped open the bottle of champagne and poured them both a glass.

"To…success," he said, raising his glass to her.

She laughed and clicked her glass against his. "To success." She took a sip of the bubbly liquid and said, "It's wonderful."

He took a sip and observed her over the rim of his glass. "You look beautiful."

She smiled with pleasure. "Thank you. So do you."

"Thank you," he said with a grin. She was normally so competent and sure of herself, but now her gaze flitted around, clearly indicating she was nervous. She finished the champagne quickly and he filled her glass again.

"Well," she said, after another sip. "Better." As she continued to glance here and there, it seemed to dawn on her that things were a little different. "Oh, you did something."

"Yes." He stood by the table and enjoyed watching her make her discoveries.

"Everything looks so nice. You have candles. Oh, and flowers. So many." She wandered over to the fireplace mantle where the largest vase of roses had been placed. "They're so pretty. Did you do all this for me?"

"You seemed to like the idea of a little romance."

"I do." Her eyes were shining and her mouth was curved in a smile he wanted to taste. "I really do."

"I aim to please," he said easily. "Let's start over here." He crossed the room to meet her halfway. Taking hold of her arm, he led her back to the table.

"Here, try some of this." He took the cover off a silver bowl filled with chocolate mousse and dipped the spoon in. He added a small dollop of whipped cream and raised it to her lips. "Tell me what you think."

"Oh. Oh." Her eyes closed as she savored the taste. Her tongue lapped at a bit of chocolate on her lip. Aidan's stomach muscles twisted in a dark coil of desire and he grew rock hard as he watched her expression turn to one of rapture. "It's heaven."

When she opened her eyes, he put the spoon down. "I'm sorry, Ellie, but there's something we need to take care of right now."

Five

"Oh," she said, blinking as if she were coming awake after a long nap. "About what? Our custody agreement? Aidan, you don't have to worry. I already took care of that. It's been signed and sent back to the lawyers."

"Good, but this has nothing to do with that. This is about…this." He took one more step closer and covered her lips with his in a kiss so tender, so sensual, so much sweeter than any chocolate, he found himself in danger of losing it right there. He clamped on tight to his control because there was no way he was stopping now.

"Just had to get that out of the way," he muttered, running his fingers along the side of her face, his desire to touch her more urgent than the need to breathe.

"Okay," she whispered and swayed a little unsteadily. "Okay. Good. Practice. Like you said. Probably a good idea, really. Makes perfect sense." She licked her lips and stared up at him.

That was enough to push Aidan into going for more. The taste of her lingered on his mouth, like a fine wine that made you thirsty for more.

He pulled her close for another kiss, then changed angles and used his tongue to urge her lips open. She wrapped her arms around his neck and pressed herself against him, her fresh scent surrounding him as her soft curves molded to his hardness. He kept his hold on her gentle while his tongue plunged and wrestled with hers in a sensuous dance that left him on a dangerous edge. He wanted to go deeper, taste more of her sweetness, more of her essence, more of everything.

"More," he murmured, and moved his hand to graze the smooth arc of her breast. His mouth returned to hers, claiming her for his own with another mind-numbing kiss so hot it felt as if he were branding her. Or maybe it was the other way around.

"Yes," she answered, holding on to his waist in an effort to press herself even closer to him. It was a possessive move that he enjoyed way too much. He wanted her even closer, but that wouldn't happen as long as they were both wearing so many clothes.

Taking a step back from her, he grabbed the hem of her top and lifted it up and off in one smooth move. She reached out and did the same with his shirt, tossing it aside.

"Better," she said greedily, and splayed her hands against his bare chest.

He laughed, but the sound emerging from his throat was raw with need. "Almost." He untied the knot at her waist and her skirt slid down her legs to pool on the floor around her feet. He held her arm to steady her as she stepped out of her clothes and slipped off her flirty sandals, ending up in only a lacy pink bra and a tiny matching thong.

"Much better," he managed to say.

As he encouraged her, she seemed to gain more confi-

dence. Now she tentatively hooked her thumbs under the thin
straps of her panties and then glanced up at him.

"Yes," he said.

She pulled them down slowly, her gaze fixed on him all
the while.

He hadn't thought he could get any more rigid, but he was
wrong. In a rush now, he grasped her petite rear with both
hands and hoisted her up into his arms. Their mouths met
in a frenzy of heat as he walked into the large master suite
with her arms clinging to his shoulders.

He knelt on the end of the bed and laid her on the cool
linen, then followed her down. With both hands, he brushed
her hair back from her face and then ran his palms along her
jaw, her throat, her shoulders. When he reached her breasts,
he cupped their warm softness and rubbed her pink nipples
with his thumbs, causing her to moan with pleasure.

"Beautiful," he whispered and bent down to take her in his
mouth, first one breast, then the other, licking, sucking and
nibbling as Ellie writhed with delight. Her hands grabbed his
shoulders and held him tightly as she moaned her approval.

Sensation soared through him like a heat-seeking mis-
sile. His body was hard and aching and he yearned to release
himself within her heated depths, but knew it was more important and ultimately more fulfilling to bring her to pleasure first. Mainly because it brought him so much pleasure
to touch her like this. Especially her breasts. He couldn't
get enough of them.

Truth be told, he'd been thinking about her for two long
days and dreaming of this moment for two damn nights.
Hell, longer really, if he was being honest. He'd spent most
of his time in California dwelling on her. And that was before he'd seen her taking that erotic shower in her bikini.

And now he couldn't get enough of her. And unless he'd
missed his mark it was obvious that Ellie felt the same way.

Okay, maybe her true motive was to get the baby she'd always wanted, but she was still enjoying herself.

He wasn't ready to think about her need for a family of her own. Right here and right now was all that mattered. This was real, he thought, as he ran his tongue over her delectable nipples. Sex was real. Ellie's lush body was real. Her staying on the island was real.

Aidan raised his head to look at her and saw her smiling at him. Something twitched in his chest, something warm and unfamiliar that was probably hazardous to his health. He would have to think about that later. Right now, the need to taste her again was overwhelming and he stretched up to meet her mouth with his in a sizzling kiss. As their tongues linked and tangled together, he slid his hand down the length of her body. Her skin was smooth and slightly damp from their exertions and he wanted to savor every inch of it.

He could feel her heart beating in time with his own, could feel her anticipation spike as he moved his hand across her thigh. As he touched her most sensitive skin, she moaned and pressed up against his hand, urging him to touch her everywhere. He strained to control his own needs, but he was on dangerous ground as he entered her warm core and heard her gasp.

"Please, Aidan, please," she said, writhing with pleasure as he stroked her, stoking her heat again and again.

He glanced up at her. "Please what, baby?"

"I want you inside me now," she cried. "Now."

With a feral grin, he moved to his knees to comply with her demand. Spreading her legs, he entered her in one swift move, covering himself to the hilt.

She gasped and clutched his shoulders. "Oh, yes."

"Oh, yeah," he muttered gutturally in response, as he thrust once again to embed himself even more deeply within her tight, lush folds. After a moment, he began to move, slowly at first, deliberately, inexorably, the sweet friction building pressure as he pushed himself into her warmth, then out.

He kissed her again, sweeping in with his tongue to parlay with hers. The provocative movement mirrored their more primal rhythms, pushing him relentlessly to the edge each time, before he was able to reel himself back with what was left of his ragged control.

She gasped with joy, giving him the strength to rally, and with one last burst of power, he plunged again, and again, impaling her with more sensual force than he'd ever been capable of before. As she screamed his name, he thrust inside her one last time, then fell to earth and into her welcoming arms.

Outside, the tropical air was hushed and still. In Aidan's room, Ellie could hear only the sound of their breathing, heavy and tattered, and the soft whirring of the ceiling fan above the bed. Despite her near exhaustion, Ellie was exhilarated. She wanted to burst into song, although most sexual etiquette books would probably frown on that.

She lay on her back and stared up at the ceiling fan, feeling dazed and confused in all the best ways. Who in a million years would've ever believed that she would wind up having incredible, mind-blowing sex with Aidan Sutherland? Not Ellie. Heck, not anyone who knew them. Yet here she was, damp, spent and completely enthralled by what they had just done together.

And before she went spiraling down into a dark place, she quickly told herself that *enthrallment* just meant that she'd had fun. That was all. It didn't mean she would suddenly become obsessed with him, for goodness sake. This was business. Or rather, pre-business.

Tonight was merely a practice run for later when she

would be ovulating, at which time she would hopefully get pregnant. But that didn't mean that what they'd done tonight didn't qualify as amazing and exciting. True, she didn't have a lot of empirical data to compare it to, but she was willing to bet that their lovemaking could match up to anyone else's on the wildest side of the wild scale.

As Aidan turned onto his side and wrapped his arms around her, her heart swelled. He had been so generous, so caring, so thoughtful. So sexy. So forceful and compelling.

She had expected sex with Aidan to be fun. She hadn't expected it to be so deep, so intense, so shattering to her heart and soul. And didn't that spell trouble? Probably so. But she figured as long as she kept the thought tucked in a corner of her mind that this was essentially a business arrangement, she knew she would be able to control her emotions.

"I can tell you're thinking too much," he murmured. "Let's have none of that."

"But it's all good thoughts," she assured him. "I feel good."

"Yes, you do," he said, rolling up onto his elbow and eyeing her as a panther would eye a doe.

Without a word, he dipped his head down and licked her breast, causing her to moan in response. He took her nipple into his mouth and tormented her with his lips, tongue and teeth.

"I have to have you again," he said.

She ran her fingers through his hair, then latched on and pressed him to her breast. "Yes, please," she said.

A while later, she struggled to lift her head off his chest. "Was that naughty sex?"

He chuckled. "Officially speaking, tonight we're featuring romantic sex."

"Romantic sex," she murmured. "I like it. Although I really think I'll like naughty sex, too."

"I'm sure you will," he said, and reached out to nip at her earlobe with his teeth. He licked the tender skin, then moved along her jawline, kissing and nibbling as he went. "Let's be sure to work on that one later in the week."

She shivered. "I'd like that." Experimenting, she reached down and stroked his length, tentatively at first, then with confidence as he grew more rigid in her hand.

"I like that, too," he muttered, gritting his teeth.

"You don't mind?" she whispered.

"I'll mind a lot more if you stop."

"Good," she said as she continued learning every inch of him. She wanted him in every way, wanted to experience more of him, all of him.

And what was wrong with that? she thought. *Want* wasn't the same as *need,* right? Right. She would simply enjoy herself for as long as she was able to. It didn't mean she was obsessed; it meant she was having fun.

Besides, enjoying herself, relaxing, was essential if she was trying to get pregnant. And pregnancy was the ultimate goal. Once she'd achieved that, she would deal with the myriad feelings and worries. For now, she would concentrate on enjoying sex with Aidan.

Stretching up to meet his gaze, she said, "I like the way you feel."

"Feeling's mutual," he was barely able to utter. And then he didn't speak at all.

An hour later, she stirred beside him.

"I should go," she whispered.

"No," he said, surprising them both.

It meant nothing, he reasoned, only that he wanted her in his bed for a while longer. Why not? Their connection was strictly physical. His heart was not engaged, only his libido. That made it okay for her to stay. At least, that's what he told himself because it couldn't be anything more than sex, right? The greatest sex of his life, for sure, but still, it was just sex.

And besides, it was just one night. Everything would go back to normal tomorrow.

"Stay," he urged, ignoring the warmth spreading through his chest, dangerously close to his heart. He wrapped his arms around her and gathered her close so that her curvy backside was pressed against him temptingly. "A few more minutes won't matter."

The next day, Aidan was too busy to leave his office so he didn't run into Ellie at all. He had hoped she would stop by at some point during the day, only because she was his right-hand man…person. They always had business to discuss.

But he didn't buzz her and ask her to come by because, well, he didn't want to seem too eager to see her. Even though, truth be told, he couldn't wait to see her again.

"Great. It's already getting weird," he muttered, scowling at his coffee mug.

He pushed away from the desk and poured himself another cup of coffee. Yeah, it was getting weird, and it was all on him.

He'd originally suggested helping Ellie out so that her child would grow up knowing its father and so he wouldn't have to run his business without her. And yeah, okay, there was that little issue of wanting Ellie in his bed more than just about anything. But now that he'd scratched that itch, so to speak, he should've been over this feeling of constant need for her. Instead, he found himself thinking about her too much, wanting her too much.

So yeah, the weirdness was all coming from him. Idiot.

"It's just sex," he said under his breath. And therein lay

the problem. He hadn't had a good, healthy bout of wild sex in a long time, so naturally, he was still thinking about it. The fact that he'd had that wild sex with *Ellie* wasn't the issue. He would've felt this way about anyone.

Good. Problem solved. He wasn't as big an idiot as he thought he was.

It was no big deal. They were both having a good time. Eventually, Ellie would get her baby. Aidan would achieve his goal of keeping her child from growing up without the support of one of his parents. And Ellie would stay on the island, which meant that the Sutherland Corporation would continue to operate at the same high level of efficiency that Aidan and Logan and their investors had come to expect.

And that meant that all of this wild sex was a win-win for everyone.

Yeah, that was his story and he was sticking to it.

Good. He'd worked it all out, so now he could get back to concentrating on business. He had a load of work to get through today and he was going to stay in the office all night if he had to in order to get it done. He didn't have time to dwell on Ellie's extremely hot body, her shapely thighs or her magnificent breasts, or the startling image of her clever hands wrapped around his—

"Stop that," he berated himself aloud. Taking in a deep, bracing breath, he let it out slowly. "Now get back to work."

Ellie re-read the custody agreement one more time. The lawyers had sent her a fully executed original and since she'd already signed it, she was satisfied with it. It was a done deal. But she still couldn't quite believe Aidan had agreed to go through with it, so she'd decided to read the document again, just to make sure. And oddly enough, just reading the legalities of what Aidan had consented to do for her made Ellie feel even closer to him, somehow. Oh, they were definitely closer now that they were having sex, and that was wonderful. But this agreement made her feel even closer to him on a vital, life-giving level.

They had agreed on many of the essential points she had listed in her slide presentation and most of those items had been integrated into this legal document. But Aidan had fought back persuasively on a few of the others. He simply hadn't been willing to relinquish all his claims to Ellie's future baby.

He wanted to be listed as the father on the child's birth certificate and Ellie was in complete agreement with that. A child should know who her father was, right? Even if that father wanted nothing to do with her.

Ellie rubbed her arms to ward off the chill that that thought brought. Even though her own father had cut off all ties with her and her sister, that didn't mean that Ellie's own child would ever experience that same level of hurt and confusion. No, her child would always know that she was completely loved and wanted by Ellie. They were a complete family, just the two of them. But now Aidan wanted to play a tiny part, too, and she had decided that that was fine. After all, once the baby was here, she didn't expect him to be much more than a friendly visitor in their lives.

But Aidan had surprised her again by requesting a more liberal visitation arrangement than she had originally proposed. Of course, since her original idea was that there be no visitation at all, no connection between her child and Aidan or his family, she supposed she couldn't blame him for asking for a little more leniency on that item.

Still, Ellie had argued with herself on that one. After all, some anonymous sperm donor wouldn't be given those rights, would they? No, of course not. But since it was Aidan and since his family was so lovely, she couldn't find it in her heart to fight him. Besides, they would all be living on

Alleria so it would be pretty hard to avoid having her child run into its father from time to time. Better to be upfront about all of this from the get-go.

But then Aidan had insisted on supporting her and her child monetarily, too. Ellie had tried to turn him down, but he had persisted. She'd pointed out that it was odd for a man who had no interest in children to be so adamant about supporting this child. Aidan had brushed it off as being something any man would do, but Ellie knew he was wrong about that.

Finally, Aidan had included a clause that stated that he intended to rewrite his will to include the child, which, in the privacy of her office, had moved Ellie to tears. She had never expected that level of generosity and support, especially from a man who, let's face it, had only offered to father her child to keep her on the island. That's what she'd originally thought, anyway. Clearly, she was wrong about him in more ways than one.

The following morning, Ellie decided that this must be her week for signing personal legal documents. Soon after she arrived at her office, her assistant dropped a thick, padded envelope on top of her inbox. It was her copy of the Sutherland partnership agreement Aidan had promised her. How he had been able to have the lawyers write it up so quickly was a mystery to her, but she'd read it over carefully, called the lawyer to clarify a few issues, then signed it the next day.

Unable to hold in her excitement, she checked that her secretary wasn't watching, then jumped in the air and clicked her heels with joy. She was now a partner in the Sutherland Corporation! She clutched the document to her heart and tried to hold back the happy tears trying to escape her eyes. It wouldn't do to burst into waterworks in the office, but this was a moment worth savoring. After all, it seemed that so many of her dreams were coming true. A fabulous career advancement, a baby someday soon, and hot sex with her fantasy man.

This called for a celebration. She brushed her hair and added a touch of lip gloss to her lips, then walked down the hall to Aidan's office.

"Are you busy?" she said when he opened the door.

"Always," he said, but since he was smiling and holding the door open, she walked in.

"I wanted to thank you," she said.

"For what?"

She threw her arms up in the air and whirled around. "It's official, I'm a partner! Thank you so much, Aidan. I won't let you down."

He stood there grinning at her, so she hugged him before she could think too much about it.

"It's probably not very businesslike, but I was sitting in my office staring at my signature on the partnership agreement, and realized I just had to share my happiness with someone. I thought of you."

"I'm happy, too, Ellie. And so is Logan. We're both thrilled to have you on board. And we know you won't let us down. You could never do that. You're our right-hand man."

"Woman," she amended.

"Person," he said, and they both laughed. It was an old routine, but she loved it.

They stared at each other in amusement for a long moment. Ellie turned speculative as Aidan's eyes turned a smoldering gray and narrowed in on her. It wasn't the first time she'd felt like she was staring into the eyes of a sexy, too-tempting-for-words predator.

They stayed frozen in place for a few charged seconds, then both of them took one step toward the other and in an instant, his mouth was covering hers in a kiss so incendiary, it was a miracle she didn't burst into flames.

He let her go, sucked in a deep breath, then ripped his jacket off and loosened his tie. As he grabbed at the buttons of his shirt, he dashed to the door, slammed it shut and locked it. "Take off your clothes."

He didn't have to ask her twice. Her shoes, gray linen slacks and pink panties were already strewn on the floor. She was halfway out of her blouse when he grabbed her and hefted her up into his arms. She wrapped her legs around his waist and they kissed again.

"This is going to be fast and hot," he warned her, his rugged body tight with coiled tension.

"Then what are you waiting for?"

He laughed, took a quick glance around and said, "Over there." He rushed her to the wall behind his desk and pressed her back up against the smooth surface.

"Take me," he muttered, holding her steady as she slid down his torso and took his hot, hard arousal inside her so deeply, she cried out.

"Did I hurt you?" he asked immediately.

"No. God, no," she assured him, her eyelids fluttering from the blissful impact. "You just feel so good."

He kissed her hungrily. "So do you."

She began the slow glide up and down, moaning as each thrust touched her more deeply, more thoroughly than anything had ever touched her before.

With her back pressed against the wall, her breasts jutted out at him, teasing him to distraction. He made a quick adjustment in order for his mouth to reach out and feast on her, feeling a hot blast of satisfaction as her nipples tightened in response. He used his tongue to lick and suck them until he had her shuddering in his arms.

He took over for her, grabbing hold of her buttocks and

holding her firmly as he plundered her moist core with hard, slow, thrusts, doubling the gratification for both of them. He moved faster, went deeper, harder, pushing into her with a savage fervor that nearly drove him to the brink of madness. His mind blanked out and pure sensation took over. When Ellie cried out his name, he buried himself inside her with one final thrust and tumbled with her into the sweet void.

Replete with pleasure, unable to move, they stood against the wall hanging on to each other like drunken sailors for several long minutes.

Aidan finally found the strength to carry Ellie across the office to the leather couch, where they sprawled beside each other in full naked splendor. Ellie didn't have the energy to cover herself, but figured Aidan wouldn't mind.

"Now that's a first," he said after a while, still trying to catch his breath.

"I take it that was naughty sex," she whispered, amazed that she was able to speak, let alone string words together to make a full sentence.

"No, that was office sex," he said, then considered his words for a moment. "Which is inherently naughty, I think."

Ellie considered their nakedness and the sight of all their clothing spread across his office carpet. She was still struggling for breath, but now she knew it wasn't just from the activity of moments before. Had a line been crossed here? Her heart was pumping faster and her throat was all tangled up. Too many emotions were zinging through her to allow her to think straight. She'd never felt anything like this before, but there was no way she could say any of that aloud. *Keep it light,* she cautioned herself. "This definitely qualifies as naughty."

He rolled over and kissed her, then reached to fondle her breasts. "Did you like it?"

"I did," she said, trembling from his touch. "I liked it very much."

"Good. Me, too," he said, easing her up and over until she was lying on top of him, bringing him back to life. "So now that we've had naughty office sex, I say we move on to *Congratulations, Partner* sex."

OFFICIAL OPINION POLL

Dear Reader,

Since you are a book enthusiast, we would like to know what you think.

Inside you will find a short Opinion Poll. Please participate in our poll by sharing your opinion on 3 subjects that are very important to all of us.

To thank you for your participation, we would like to send you **2 FREE BOOKS** and **2 FREE GIFTS!**

Please enjoy them with our compliments.

Sincerely,

Pam Powers

For Your Reading Pleasure...

Get 2 FREE BOOKS with rich, powerful heros and scandalous family sagas.

Free

Your **2 FREE BOOKS** have a combined cover price of $10.00 in the U.S. and $12.00 in Canada.

Peel off sticker and place by your completed poll on the right page and you'll automatically receive **2 FREE BOOKS** and **2 FREE GIFTS** with no obligation to purchase anything!

YOUR OPINION POLL
THANK-YOU FREE GIFTS INCLUDE:

▶ **2 HARLEQUIN DESIRE® BOOKS**
▶ **2 LOVELY SURPRISE GIFTS**

OFFICIAL OPINION POLL

YOUR OPINION COUNTS!
Please check TRUE or FALSE below to express your opinion about the following statements:

Q1 Do you believe in "true love"?

"TRUE LOVE HAPPENS ONLY ONCE IN A LIFETIME."
○ TRUE
○ FALSE

Q2 Do you think marriage has any value in today's world?

"YOU CAN BE TOTALLY COMMITTED TO SOMEONE WITHOUT BEING MARRIED."
○ TRUE
○ FALSE

Q3 What kind of books do you enjoy?

"A GREAT NOVEL MUST HAVE A HAPPY ENDING."
○ TRUE
○ FALSE

YES! I have placed my sticker in the space provided below. Please send me the **2 FREE books** and **2 FREE gifts** for which I qualify. I understand that I am under no obligation to purchase anything further, as explained on the back of this card.

225/326 HDL FVPJ

FIRST NAME

LAST NAME

ADDRESS

APT.#

CITY

STATE/PROV.

ZIP/POSTAL CODE

HD-TF-03/13
Printed in the U.S.A.
© 2012 HARLEQUIN ENTERPRISES LIMITED.

Six

Aidan and Ellie had been sleeping together for a week when Logan and his new bride returned from their honeymoon.

The following day was Logan's first day back at work. He was sitting at Aidan's desk checking the computer while Aidan riffled through the file cabinet on the far wall, when Ellie walked in.

"Welcome back, Logan," Ellie said cheerfully, and rounded the desk to give him a hug before dropping a document on the desk. "I hope you and Grace had a wonderful honeymoon."

"It was fantastic."

"I'm so happy for you," she said, then turned to Aidan. "I'm making that New York phone call in thirty minutes."

"Thank you."

Both men watched her walk out of the office; then Aidan said, "I know we talked about offering Ellie the partnership when you got back, but something came up while you were gone. I made her the offer last week and she accepted."

Logan frowned at Aidan. "Did you notice that Ellie knew it was me sitting here?"

"So?" Aidan said absently as he picked up the document Ellie had delivered.

Logan glanced down at his dark navy business suit, burgundy silk tie and white shirt, then stared across at his brother, who wore the same basic outfit. "I'm sitting at your desk, dressed exactly like you. Anyone in the company would think I *was* you. But Ellie knew it was me."

Aidan gave him a sideways glance. "Ellie's smart. She's been able to tell us apart from day one. No big deal."

Logan stared long and hard at Aidan. "Oh, hell. You're having sex with her! Are you out of your mind?"

Aidan scowled and told himself he never should have let his brother walk into his office. "Where the hell did you get that idea?"

"We're twins, remember?" Logan said. "I can read you like a book. A really *stupid* book with a lousy plotline."

"Get serious." Aidan's gaze slid from his twin's. He never had been able to hide a damn thing from Logan. But damned if he was going to stand here and be lectured. "There's nothing going on. How in the hell did you come up with sex?"

"Easy," Logan said as he pulled two small bottles of sparkling water from the small refrigerator in the credenza along the wall. He popped the tops, handed one to Aidan and walked back to the desk. "And I'm right, too, so stop pretending it's not true."

Aidan took a long gulp of water and tried to figure out why he'd been so anxious for Logan to get home.

His brother wasn't finished ranting. "And what was that about offering Ellie the partnership? Don't you remember we talked about doing it together when I got back from my trip? You couldn't wait?"

"I told you, something came up," Aidan muttered.

"Yeah, I know exactly what came up," Logan said with an evil smirk.

"That's not what I mean," he said, and grabbed a bag of chips from the supplies cupboard to munch on.

A few minutes ago, Aidan had been pleased to see Logan at his office door. He and Grace had been back on the island since the day before, but Aidan hadn't had a chance to talk to Logan until this morning. But right now, Aidan was kind of wishing his brother would take off for another week or two.

This was the problem with being a twin. He couldn't get a damn thing past his brother.

Annoyed with the direction their conversation was heading, Aidan paced back and forth across the office floor. Finally he turned to his brother and explained things in a reasonable tone of voice. "Ellie was making plans to leave the island for a few weeks. I had to do something to stop her."

"So you slept with her?" Logan shook his head. "That was your plan?"

"No. I mean, yes. But that's not why." He scraped his fingers across his scalp in frustration. "It's a long story."

Logan sat in one of the comfortable visitor's chairs and stretched out his long legs. "I've got all day."

Aidan huffed out a breath. "It's complicated."

"Dude, it wasn't complicated until you slept with her."

Irritation spiked. Yeah, he and Logan had always talked together about the women in their lives. But he didn't like Logan talking about Ellie. "Just shut up about that, will you?"

"She's an employee," Logan pointed out. "You're putting the company in a bad position. What if she sues you? Did you consider the possible consequences? You know she could—"

"Stop." Aidan held up his hand. "I'll ignore the fact that

you slept with Grace when she was working here as a cocktail waitress."

He was happy to see his brother frown as that realization sunk into his thick skull.

"She was a fake waitress," Logan mumbled.

"Right. Look, Ellie's a partner now, not an employee. But just in case you're still worried, don't be. She and I signed a contract before we did anything."

Logan jumped up from his chair and gaped at his brother. "What did you say? You signed a contract for sex? What the hell is going on around here?"

"What the hell do you have to be mad about?" Aidan shouted. "This isn't about you."

"If it's about Sutherland, then it's about me, too, you idiot."

"Fine." Aidan scrubbed one hand across his face, took a swig of water and muttered, "The contract wasn't about sex, all right? It's for a baby."

Logan opened his mouth to retort, but no words came out. He took a breath, blew it out and then blinked a few times as if his twin was just a hallucination he was trying to bring into focus. Funny. Aidan had never actually seen Logan speechless. He kind of liked it.

"Well, that shut you up anyway." Aidan handed him the bag of potato chips and continued his pacing.

A full minute later, Logan found his voice again. "I think you'd better sit down and tell me the whole story."

"That went well," Aidan muttered at the end of the day. What with all the interruptions and conference calls and business meetings, his conversation with Logan had stretched out over the entire day, and Logan had just left the office to take Grace to dinner. He'd invited Aidan to join them, but Aidan had declined. He had too much to think about. So instead, he went and grabbed a cheeseburger and fries from the bar, then headed back to his place to watch a football game.

He took a bite of the perfectly prepared burger and savored the flavors, marveling that he still had an appetite after hashing it out with his brother. Aidan had patiently explained everything to Logan. He had defended himself valiantly, making it clear that desperate times called for heroic efforts and that's why Aidan had finally decided to help Ellie get pregnant.

His brother hadn't seen it quite the same way. Far from it, in fact. Not to put too fine a point on it, but Logan had basically laughed his fool ass off.

"Heroic efforts?" he'd said derisively. "Man, you're killing me."

"I mean it," Aidan had insisted. "How else could I guarantee that she'd stay here and work for us? I fell on my sword, man. I made the ultimate sacrifice for the corporation."

He frowned at that, because as swords went, Ellie was a pretty damn good one. And it wasn't as if he'd had to suffer to keep their most valued employee at the resort.

Logan snorted, not an attractive sound. "You *sacrificed* yourself by having sex with Ellie? How the hell is that a sacrifice? She's gorgeous! You like her."

"Wha— Of course I like her," he sputtered. "A lot. She's a good friend. She wants to have a baby and I want that baby to know its father. I wasn't going to let her go off to some sperm bank and then raise a kid all on her own."

Logan chuckled. "Oh man, you've got it bad. Hell, you've been half in love with her ever since she started working here."

Aidan's eyes narrowed on his brother. "What did you just say?"

"Oh, just admit it," Logan said, ignoring Aidan's threatening glare. "Remember when you introduced her to that idiot Blake, then got completely pissed off when they started dating? You're so transparent, it's ridiculous. So now you're finally sleeping with her. It's not such a stretch to predict that you'll fall in love with her. Especially if you have a child together."

Aidan had to shake his head a few times to make sure his ears were really hearing those words. "Okay, you just went off the deep end, bro."

"Say whatever you want in your own defense," Logan drawled. "But I'm telling you, you did all this because you love her."

Ridiculous.

Seriously, it was sad to see how fast Logan's brain had turned to sludge after his wedding.

"Oh, man. Oh, no. Dude, you're pathetic," Aidan had said, hanging his head in sorrow. "Barely one day back from your honeymoon and you're already deluded into thinking the whole world's in love. Birdies singing in the trees, rainbows dancing in the sky, unicorns frolicking in the jungle. Snap out of it, man. You're embarrassing both of us."

Logan held up both hands. "I'm just telling it like I see it."

"I'd get my vision checked if I were you."

Logan had laughed uproariously and shortly after that, he'd taken off to meet Grace.

It was a new low in brotherly accusations, Aidan thought as he took another bite of his fully loaded cheeseburger. He still couldn't believe his own brother had charged him with being in love with Ellie. It was worse than pitiable. It was a sad, sad cliché. Now that Logan had gone and gotten married, he wanted everyone else to be in love. Well, good luck with that.

Aidan shook his head again, feeling nothing but sorry for

Logan. He felt sorry for Grace, too, because his brother was clearly in need of psychiatric care.

On the other hand, he mused, Logan was right about one thing. Ellie was gorgeous. Of course, Logan had no idea just how gorgeous since he wasn't the one who'd seen her in that bikini. A good thing, too, because Aidan would have to kill him if he had.

That had nothing to do with love, by the way, he assured himself. That was just pure male defensive action. No man wanted other guys checking out the woman he was… Aidan frowned. The woman he was currently having sex with. Right. That's all it was.

The image of Ellie in her dripping wet bikini halted his thought process for a few minutes before he managed to get his mind back to the subject at hand. Logan and his wacko thinking.

Yes, his brother was right when he said that Aidan *liked* Ellie. Why wouldn't he? They had worked together closely for four years now, and Ellie traveled with Aidan any time they went to meet with investors. The two of them agreed on almost everything and had a great time together whenever they traveled together. Negotiations were always more fun when Ellie was there with him. Aidan loved watching her come up with all sorts of obscure facts and figures in an instant to impress the investors and their accountants.

Okay, Aidan didn't actually mean that he *loved* watching her do those tricks with numbers. He just meant that he *liked* it. He was *impressed* and *entertained* by her. That's all. He didn't mean *love*, as in *I love you*. He just meant…

"Oh hell, enough already," he muttered, and stuffed a French fry into his mouth. "Chill out. Jeez."

This was all Logan's fault. His brother had wigged out over the whole *love* issue and now Aidan was second-guessing every last word in his head.

Funny how Logan was the big "love expert" these days, considering that both of them had once felt the same way about that useless emotion. Part of their cynicism had come from the complete lack of love their mother had shown them and their father. But their scorn had grown with their life on the surfing circuit, where every woman they'd met had seemed more than willing to pledge her eternal love just to get close to the celebrated twin brothers. Love was a joke.

Hell, his brother had been even more scornful about love than Aidan, considering that the one time Logan had actually convinced himself he was in love, he'd gone and married a woman who had cheated on him to her dying day. She'd put on a good show, but she hadn't known the meaning of love, never mind commitment and faithfulness.

Of course, once Grace had come into Logan's life, he'd changed his mind about all of it. Grace was the real thing, and Aidan couldn't blame his brother for falling in love with her. But did that mean that Aidan had to follow in lockstep? Why would he bother to fall in love with one woman when he could have his choice of so many? It was a no-brainer.

Lately, of course, the only woman he was interested in was Ellie. They were having a good time together and would continue to do so as long as it lasted. Didn't mean he was in love, despite his brother's deranged insistence.

He never should've said anything to Logan. He had a feeling he was going to regret that lapse in judgment for a long time.

"Hell, I *love* this burger," Aidan exclaimed scornfully. Then he popped the last juicy bite into his mouth. "There. See? That's true love for you."

It was early in the morning two days later when Ellie walked to the office and came upon Grace digging in the hard sand around the base of a coco palm tree. The research scientist was dressed for gardening and wore a straw hat with a wide brim to protect her from the strong rays of the sun.

Ellie had become friends with Grace through Serena and Dee, a waitress who worked in the bar. Ellie called out a greeting and Grace waved, then jumped up to give her a hug.

"I haven't seen you in ages," Grace said. "Not since we got back from our honeymoon."

"I don't have to ask if you had a good time," Ellie said. "I can tell just by looking at you."

"It was heavenly," Grace admitted. "But I'll tell you all about it when we girls get together this weekend."

"Can't wait to hear all the details," Ellie said, then glanced around at the trees. "Are you out here hunting for more spores?"

Everyone knew that Grace had come to the island originally to collect the rare Allerian spores for her research. That's when she'd met Logan and they'd fallen in love.

"Yes, this area of the grove is riddled with the little darlings," Grace said, and glanced up at the sky. "Morning's the best time to find them, before the sun gets too hot. I've done all I can do today."

Ellie knew Grace loved her spores, and who could blame her? The Allerian spores had provided the means by which she had discovered several new methods for treating some of the worst diseases known to mankind.

"I'm so glad," Ellie said. "And I heard that your laboratory is almost finished."

"It is." Grace grinned. "Logan added a generous bonus to the deal if the men could get it finished ahead of schedule, so it'll be ready to move in next week. I'm thrilled, as you can imagine, and Logan went out and bought every piece of lab equipment ever created, so I can't wait to get to work."

"That's wonderful," Ellie said. "Your research is so important and it's such an honor to have you here with us."

"Oh, aren't you sweet?" Grace said. She glanced down at the ground where she'd left a basket filled with gloves and lab supplies. "Will you wait while I gather up my stuff? I'll walk with you to the office."

"I'd like that."

A minute later, the two women were headed toward the executive offices at the resort. Grace frowned thoughtfully at her friend. "You look different, Ellie."

"I do?" Ellie said, and laughed. "I'm not sure how to take that. Good different or bad different?"

"Definitely good," Grace assured her. "You look really happy."

"Do I?" Ellie said softly. "I guess that's because I am."

"It must be because of Aidan. Oh!" Grace slapped her hand over her mouth. "That's none of my business."

"I don't mind," Ellie said. "The island is like a small town, isn't it? Everyone knows everyone else's business. But I love it. And I like that I have friends who care about me enough to gossip behind my back."

Grace's eyes widened. "Oh, Ellie, we didn't... I mean, we wouldn't... Oh, dear. I'm embarrassed."

Ellie burst out laughing. "Are you kidding? Don't be. I love it. I didn't have many friends growing up, so now that I do, I love everything that goes along with having friends. Including gossip."

"Oh, but that's just wrong."

"Maybe," Ellie said, "but do you honestly believe we didn't talk about you while you were gone?"

Grace laughed. "I certainly hope you did. And you know, I don't mind at all. As long as nothing too vicious was said."

Ellie patted Grace's arm. "No one could ever say a vicious word about you."

"Same goes for you. I got your back, girlfriend."

They smiled in complete harmony.

"So that's cleared up," Grace said. "Now let's hear all about Aidan. What happened when. And how and why and where. Start at the beginning and don't stop until I've heard all the pertinent details."

Ellie laughed. She was so lucky to have girlfriends after so many years of hiding from people, that now she had no qualms at all about telling Grace everything. She told her about her spur-of-the-moment decision to start a family and the sperm bank and Aidan's offer and how she'd decided to take him up on it.

"I must say I agree with you on that point," Grace said. "A big, handsome man in the flesh beats the heck out of an anonymous turkey baster any day of the week."

"And Aidan is so wonderful," Ellie confided. "I'm seeing a side of him I never knew existed. He's funny and caring and kind and…well, I guess I knew he was all that, but it just seems that the more time I spend with him, the more I care about him."

She didn't add that it worried her, but it did. Her feelings seemed to grow stronger every day and if she wasn't careful, the little crush she'd always had on him could develop into a full-on love that she would never recover from. Just like her mother. It was the stupidest thing Ellie could possibly allow to happen.

And in case she'd forgotten, as soon as she became pregnant, their temporary situation would be over. Aidan wouldn't need to be with her anymore. There would be no reason to see him except during regular business hours. And though she knew it was for the best, that brought a little ache to Ellie's heart.

She'd known going into the deal that Aidan had no intention of going beyond what they'd agreed to do. Once she was pregnant, he would go back to dating the bikini babes who came to the island looking for some short-term action.

Aidan didn't believe in long-term relationships. He'd made that clear from the very beginning.

So right then and there, she renewed her vow to stay strong in the face of those feelings that could destroy her. Still, a tiny wishful part of her was just as determined to keep the dream going for as long as possible and pretend that she and Aidan were more than just temporary lovers.

She suddenly remembered it was Grace she was talking to and quickly added, "Oh, but Logan is wonderful, too, Grace. I just never had as much of a connection with him as I do with Aidan."

"I'm glad to hear it," Grace said with a light laugh. "Otherwise, I would've had to kill you."

At noon a few days later, Ellie walked down the hall to Logan's office, where she would join the brothers for their first private partners' lunch. Ellie was relieved that ever since Logan had returned from his honeymoon, he had welcomed her into the partnership with open arms.

Once they were seated and the catering crew had served their crab salads, Logan held up his glass of sparkling water and toasted her. "Welcome to the penthouse suite, Ellie."

"Yes, welcome," Aidan said. "Of course, since we're on the first floor you can't take that too literally."

It didn't really matter, Ellie thought, glancing around. Logan's office was the mirror image of Aidan's and was essentially a large hotel suite. It was furnished in a casually elegant style with modern furniture arranged to form a comfortable conversation area at one end of the room with a fully functioning office at the other. In between was a conference table and chairs where they were seated for their lunch.

The best part of the room was the view. One entire wall of sliding glass doors opened onto a private terrace. The view beyond the terrace was of the white sand beach and blue water of the bay. Graceful coco palm trees swayed in the breeze.

As the three of them began to eat, Logan led the conversation. "I don't know if Aidan told you, but we've been thinking of making you a partner for months now. Right before I left for my honeymoon, we decided to take care of it as soon as I got back."

"I told her," Aidan admitted to Logan, then flashed Ellie a half smile. "Before he left on his honeymoon, we talked about the fact that he would be gone for three weeks. That can be a long time in this business. It got us thinking that it was time to bring someone in who knows the business as well as we do and who we respect and have complete confidence in."

"That's you, Ellie," Logan said.

"Thank you, Logan," she said. She hadn't thought about it until that moment, but it was no wonder she'd received the partnership agreement so quickly. The lawyers had probably had it written up and waiting for the past few weeks.

"No, thank you," Logan insisted. "We consider you an essential part of the team."

"I consider myself that, too. Thank you both for placing your trust in me. I won't let you down."

"You never have," Aidan said, watching her closely.

She took a deep breath and let it out slowly. "Well, I can only take these compliments for another hour or so, then I think we should get to work."

The men laughingly agreed and soon they were dealing with Logan's agenda for the next six months. First new business was a time-share project they planned to discuss with their investors next month. It would mean a trip to New York and Ellie's mind wandered to an image of her and Aidan spending a romantic weekend in New York City. Walks in Central Park, a romantic dinner at—

"Ellie can handle that right away," Aidan said.

"Good." Logan nodded as he read over his agenda and made notes. "Cross that off the list. What's next?"

"What?" Ellie said, suddenly aware that she'd missed an entire agenda item. "Handle…sure, I can do that. Um, what?" Good grief! Ellie wanted to crawl out of the room. This was so not a good time to turn into a flake. She cleared her throat, tapped her pen on the table surface and tried to sound businesslike. "I apologize. I was trying to calculate what size advance team we'll need to line up for the New York trip." She turned to Aidan. "Exactly what would you like me to handle?"

The look he gave her was provocative enough to make her squirm in her chair. Had she really asked that question out loud? Double entendre, anyone?

"I'd like you to *handle* the Bryson project," Aidan said softly, his subtext unashamedly obvious. To Ellie, at least. She only hoped Logan was too busy taking notes to notice.

Was this tingling, yearning feeling going to crop up every time she was in the same office with Aidan? How would she ever get her work done? Would Logan regret offering her the partnership if he caught her making moon eyes at his brother whenever they sat at the same conference table together? Good grief. She had to straighten up and get back to business. Otherwise, she was doomed.

Twenty minutes later, the lunch meeting ended and Ellie couldn't run out of there fast enough.

Two weeks later on a Saturday morning, Ellie paced barefoot on the cool tile floor of her sunny kitchen, waiting, watching, wondering how five minutes could seem like six hours when one was anticipating that a little pink cross might appear in the window of the pregnancy test stick.

But five minutes passed and there was no cross. Ten minutes later, she checked again. No cross. No nothing.

So she wasn't pregnant.

"Okay," she whispered, tossing the stick into the trash can under the sink. "Just means we'll have to keep trying."

Naturally, a big part of her was disappointed to know there was no tiny person starting to grow inside her. But she tried to be philosophical about it. She would get pregnant when it was meant to happen.

It wasn't like she hadn't been trying hard enough. That wasn't the issue. In fact, the opposite was true. She and Aidan had been almost fanatical in their effort to accomplish their mission by having sex as often as possible over the past few weeks. By now Ellie should've been exhausted and ready to call it quits, but she wasn't crazy. There was no way she was about to stop having sex with Aidan.

At the very thought of Aidan with his broad shoulders, dark blue eyes, windswept hair and long legs stalking across the office to yank her into his strong arms and ravish her, Ellie felt a tingle of excitement zing across her shoulders and down her spine. Another flashing image had him sliding his talented hands along her sensitive skin as his tongue brushed over her breasts, and that tingle burst into a thousand tiny jolts of electricity that zigzagged everywhere throughout her body and caused her knees to turn weak.

"Oh, my," she murmured as she stumbled to sit down at her kitchen table. This would probably be a good time to call Aidan to request that he drop by her house as soon as possible. To work. On their mission. Immediately.

Call her insatiable, but Ellie was having the time of her life. And while the lines might have started to blur between her serious mission to become pregnant and her giddiness over Aidan's stated desire to find new and inventive ways to have sex with her, she certainly appreciated his devotion to her cause. More than that, she appreciated all the thrilling new experiences he'd introduced her to.

She'd never had sex up against a wall before, for instance. Or on a conference room table. Or on the deck of a catamaran in the middle of Alleria Bay. Or on a chaise longue by the pool at midnight.

That tingle was back and her heart was starting to beat a little faster. And in case she started to worry, she reminded herself that she wasn't obsessed with Aidan. She was just having great sex with a gorgeous man. Nothing wrong with that. She wasn't turning into her mother; she was simply enjoying this wonderful time with Aidan.

So she refused to feel sorry for herself for not having accomplished her objective to be pregnant just yet. In fact, she was excited to be able to continue with their sexual encounters. She would just have to remember to ask Aidan to try a little harder the next time.

Seven

Aidan stood at the end of the long bar nursing a scotch as he watched his team of bartenders racing to keep up with the customers. The music was pumped up and so was the boisterous crowd. That's the way Aidan liked it. Friday nights were always a little crazy in the bar since many of the resort guests had just arrived that afternoon for a week of fun. But tonight was especially insane because this was the start of the annual cardboard box convention. And those people were more than ready to party.

Three years ago, Aidan and Logan had discovered a shocking truth. There was no bigger group of wild, raucous party animals than this horde of almost one thousand cardboard box salesmen. Cardboard. Go figure.

The group used to have their convention in different cities every year, but once they found Alleria and met Ellie, that all changed. Now the group refused to go anywhere else. Ellie lavished so much special attention on them that the group was back for the third year in a row.

The box boys, as Aidan and Logan referred to them in private, were one of Ellie's special projects. Attracting new business to the resort had been part of her job description from day one, and bringing the box boy convention to Alleria was one of her first successes.

The group's presence here this week was just one of many reasons why Aidan hadn't wanted her to leave the island when she first announced her plans to go to Atlanta.

Now, as he observed Ellie interacting with a small group of conventioneers gathered at the bar, Aidan was doubly glad he'd convinced her to stay. Glad, because not only could she charm these guys into spending more money on drinks, but also because Aidan could have her in his bed every night.

Not that he was getting used to her being there, he quickly assured himself. He knew it would all end when she became pregnant. But in the meantime, how could he complain about having awesome sex with a beautiful woman like Ellie every night? Hell, he wasn't that big of an idiot, despite what his brother occasionally thought.

In fact, as he watched Ellie work the crowd and as he marveled at what an amazing businesswoman she was, he was tempted to congratulate himself for coming up with the deal that had kept her on the island in the first place.

The truth was, he'd only stopped in to have a drink because he knew that Ellie would be here, taking care of her special guests. Now that he was seeing her surrounded by those men, smiling and talking and joking with them, all he could think about was getting her out of here and taking her somewhere private. It took everything he had to keep from stalking across the floor, sweeping her up into his arms and carrying her off into the night.

Just then, one of the box boys said something that must've

been funny because Ellie threw back her head and laughed. The sweet musical sound set off a shock wave of desire that shot straight to Aidan's gut. And instantly turned him as hard as a brick.

Damn. He gripped his glass carefully as he struggled to maintain an outer calm. He gritted his teeth and mentally talked himself down, but it wasn't easy because he couldn't seem to tear his gaze away from Ellie, who was still smiling and chatting easily with the men. That was just one more reason why she was so perfect for this job. She was friendly and could get along with anyone.

But that wasn't helping his erection disappear.

The music in the club pounded; laughter from the customers at the table seemed harsher, louder. Aidan kept his gaze fixed on Ellie with such intensity that she must have felt it. She turned her head, her gaze caught his and something wild and indefinable jumped into life between them.

He downed the last of his drink, set his empty glass on the bar, nodded to Sam the bartender, and headed straight toward the group of men who were vying for Ellie's attention.

Ellie had felt Aidan's presence within a nanosecond of him walking into the bar twenty minutes ago. Even with her back to the entrance, even surrounded by all these people, she knew he was here. So what did it say about her that she could sense the man's presence from across a large, crowded room?

It worried her, frankly. Would it always be this way? Was it a good thing or a bad thing? Probably bad, if it meant that in a few years, she would be at home feeding her baby and suddenly realize instinctively that Aidan was out on a date with his latest "bikini babe."

Yes, definitely a bad thing, she thought, as she recalled one night when she and her sister had watched their mother wander through the house, wondering and worrying aloud about the man she'd once been married to. What was he doing right now? Was he thinking of her?

Ellie mentally rolled her eyes. There was no way she would turn into that woman!

With a sigh, she tried to ignore all thoughts of Aidan and concentrate on the salesmen who were currently trying to impress her with all their best stories. She didn't mind. They were nice guys, if a bit silly.

A few minutes later, they moved on from stories to jokes, and Ellie had to admit some of them were mildly amusing. Then out of the blue, one of the salesmen—was his name Larry?—told a knock-knock joke that was so funny, she laughed out loud.

"Hey, she liked that one," Larry said, wiggling his eyebrows at his friends.

One of his buddies nudged him with his elbow. "Guess that means the next round of drinks is on you."

She felt Aidan's gaze on her and when she turned her head to meet that look head-on, her entire system jump-started into a frantic rhythm. Her heartbeat thundered in time with the pulsing music. Her stomach did a quick spin and at the very core of her, she went hot and damp.

She swallowed hard when he stalked toward her.

"Good evening, gentlemen," Aidan said jovially. "Hope you don't mind, but I've got to borrow our Ms. Sterling for a few minutes."

She smiled her apologies. There was some good-natured grumbling as Aidan took Ellie's arm and guided her out from the circle of men. He smiled cheerfully the entire time, although Ellie could sense his underlying tension.

"No worries, gentlemen," he said. "You'll see Ellie again tomorrow. Enjoy your evening."

"Aidan, what's wrong?" Ellie asked.

He kept a firm hold on her arm as they walked quickly through the bar and out into the bustling lobby. He paid no attention to the bell captain or the concierge director who both called out his name, just kept walking across the marble floor and into the carpeted hallway that led to his suite.

"You're scaring me, Aidan," she said, hurrying her steps to keep up with his much longer stride. "Is everything all right?"

"Sorry," he muttered. "Everything's fine. I'm just in kind of a hurry."

"Okay," she said, and practically jogged to keep up with him.

They reached his suite and without a word, he swiped his key card, pushed the door open and urged her inside. As soon as the door shut, he tugged her up against his chest and kissed her hard on the lips. The impact was sudden and startling and hot and Ellie couldn't get enough of him. She wrapped her arms around his neck and pulled him even closer to her.

Within seconds, he softened the kiss and she sighed, parting her lips to allow him entrance. Their tongues tangled gently and Ellie felt herself melting against him.

Without a warning, he stepped back, grabbed hold of her light summer dress and whipped it up and over her head, tossing it onto the chair.

Wearing only her bra and panties, Ellie grabbed his shirt and started unbuttoning it with frantic urgency.

"You're overdressed," she groused.

"Let me do it," he said, laughing as he pushed her hands away. After ripping it off his shoulders, he hoisted her into his arms and carried her through the living room and into the bedroom. He tossed her on the bed, knelt above her and unzipped his jeans, releasing his enormous erection.

Ellie shivered as he gripped her bottom, lifted her up

off the mattress and guided her onto his thick length. She groaned in pure delight as he filled her completely.

His mouth devoured hers as they moved together rhythmically and Ellie was so lost in passion, she wondered if she had been created for this moment. As his fervor met hers, they reached the pinnacle together and tumbled into rapture. Her heart was so full, she knew she had never felt so much pleasure, so much love before.

Moments later, he collapsed onto her. After catching his breath, he finally murmured in her ear, "I'm sorry I dragged you out of the bar, but I knew I was going to explode if I couldn't be inside you right away."

"I loved it," she whispered, then cringed. She only hoped her voice sounded casual saying those words. But even if Aidan wasn't spooked by the words, Ellie was. The *L* word was something she never said out loud.

But Aidan was already asleep, so she held him in her arms and they dozed for a while. Sometime in the middle of the night, Aidan woke her up and made love to her slowly. Afterwards, they slept. The next time Ellie awoke, it was morning. The sun was streaming into Aidan's bedroom, but she was alone in his bed.

She sat up, looked around and told herself that she preferred it this way. The sooner she got pregnant and got used to her life without Aidan, the better off she would be.

Hours later, Ellie sat in the bar, chatting with the friendly box boys while Larry, the funny salesman, designed a one-of-a-kind cardboard box for her on his tablet.

When he was finished, he held the screen up so she could see it. "There, just for you. I'm calling it the Ellie. Wait, we can add a design, too."

He tapped his fingers on the sidebar and the box was suddenly filled with a green and red circle pattern surrounded by curlicues.

"Oh, I like that pattern," she said, fascinated by everything he'd done. Who knew the cardboard box guys could be so creative?

"Hi, Ellie."

The deep voice came from behind her. She turned and her eyes widened in surprise at the sight of the tall, good-looking man. "Blake? What're you doing here?"

"Just thought I'd stop in for a drink and I saw you." He glanced around. "Can you take a break and talk?"

"Umm, of course." She turned back to her salesman. "I'm sorry, Larry, but would you excuse me?"

"Sure, Ellie," Larry said, eyeing Blake curiously. "No problem."

She sucked in a bracing breath and tried to mask her distress at the fact that Blake was here unannounced, then gazed up at her ex-boyfriend. "Let's go out to the terrace."

He followed her to a quiet corner of the patio bar and found an empty table. He pulled a chair out for her and as he was sitting, she took the time to study him. He was classically tall, dark and handsome, with dark brown eyes and nearly black hair. Most women would swoon over his movie-star good looks, but Ellie had learned the hard way that looks weren't everything. Not that Blake had hurt her irreparably, but he hadn't turned out to be as nice or as honorable as she'd hoped he would be.

"Would you two like something to drink?"

Ellie looked up and saw Dee, her waitress friend, standing there, looking back and forth from Ellie to Blake.

"Maybe just a glass of water," Ellie said gratefully. "Thanks, Dee."

Blake ordered a beer and Dee was back in less than two

minutes with their orders. "Let me know if you need anything else," she said pointedly.

"I will," Ellie said, smiling up at her friend.

As soon as Dee was out of hearing distance, Blake spoke. "You're looking good, Ellie."

"Thank you. I feel good."

"I wasn't sure if I'd run into you here tonight, but I'm glad I did. I've been doing a lot of thinking. About us. I know I hurt you when I broke up with you, but I was... I don't know, confused, I guess. You shocked me."

"I know, and I'm sorry." She smiled ruefully. "It wasn't fair of me to spring my life story on you."

"I guess I asked for it," he said with a sheepish grin.

She chuckled lightly. "Yes, you did."

He relaxed back in his chair and sipped his beer. "So I hear you're seeing one of the Sutherland brothers. Is it serious?"

Her eyes narrowed. Was that why Blake was here? Was she suddenly more appealing to him now that she was involved with Aidan? And how had he found out about her relationship with Aidan? The island was like a small town, but they had been very discreet, she thought. "We're good friends, that's all."

He surprised her by leaning forward and taking hold of her hand. "If that's true, then I'd like you to consider giving me another chance. I thought we had a good thing going until you laid that bombshell on me."

"Until I told you I wanted to have a child."

"Yeah." He shrugged. "But, hey, if that's what you want, I'm willing to help you out there."

Not if he were the last man on earth, she thought as she pulled her hand away. "That's very kind of you to offer, but I think I'll pass."

"So you are sleeping with Sutherland."

She smiled tightly. "I didn't say that."

He chuckled. "You didn't have to. If you're not interested in getting back with me, then I have to assume you're doing the horizontal bop with him."

The horizontal bop? Was this guy in high school or something? Aidan had been so right about Blake. He was kind of a jerk. She was lucky she'd never had to see this side of him.

Ellie pushed her chair out and stood looking down at him. "Your assumption is wrong, Blake. My refusal to get back together with you has nothing to do with anything but the fact that I'm just not interested. See you around."

Aidan couldn't believe it. He'd seen Ellie leading Blake out to this deserted area of the terrace, so he followed them, remaining back behind a thick, vine-strewn column in order to watch them. It was too bad he couldn't get close enough to hear their conversation.

He refused to question why he even cared except to say that he was worried about Ellie. So that's why he was loitering in the area. Okay, maybe *skulking* would be a more accurate description, but why quibble? He'd never liked Blake for so many reasons and here was another one. The guy was holding Ellie's hand. What the hell? There was no way Ellie could be fooled by his good looks. The guy was a creep.

Maybe she agreed because at that moment, she slipped her hand away from his, then stood and walked away.

But why was she smiling? She shouldn't be smiling after talking to Blake.

Aidan rounded the column and stepped out just as she was about to walk past him. "Hello, there."

She stopped abruptly. "What're you doing out here?"

"Just checking the foliage," he said, brushing his hand along the flowering vine. He nodded toward Blake, who had taken off in the opposite direction. "What did he want?"

Ellie planted both hands on her hips. "Were you spying on me?"

"Maybe. I warned you what he was like. He's a jerk. He's not good enough for you."

"I never said he was."

"You were holding hands with him."

"He grabbed my hand and I pulled it back."

"Not right away."

"Don't be ridiculous," she said. She moved closer, touched his chest and smiled up at him so sweetly that his jaw muscles began to loosen up. "Did you come out here to protect me?"

"I told you he was a jerk," he grumbled. "I came out here to make sure he didn't pull a number on you."

"That was very nice of you, Aidan," she said. "But you and I aren't really a couple, remember? I have to take care of myself. Thank you, though."

"No problem," he murmured, then leaned in and whispered, "And we might not be a real couple, but if Blake had held your hand a second longer, I was going to have to break his arm."

The next day, Ellie spent the day alone, cleaning her house, dusting shelves and scrubbing floors. She did a few loads of laundry and swept her front porch. Afterward, she got caught up on her reading and took a short nap. She realized she needed some rest after so many long nights waking up and making love with Aidan.

Not that she was complaining, she thought, grinning with happiness.

She hadn't seen Blake since the night before and that was fine with her. If she never saw him again, that would be even finer. She just had to wonder why Blake had shown up at all. Why now? Not that it mattered, but still, she hated the thought that she and Aidan might be a source of gossip on the island.

She woke up from her nap as the sun was going down and thought about going over to the hotel bar to grab a quick dinner. But that would mean washing her hair and dressing up, so after weighing her choices, she decided to stay home and relax. She made herself a healthy salad for dinner, then picked up her book and tried to read, but she couldn't get back into the story. She kept picturing Aidan stepping out from behind that column. He'd been watching her and Blake! He'd kept his explanation casual, but Ellie hadn't been fooled. She'd seen a fierce possessiveness in him that she'd never seen before. Did it come merely from the fact that she was his partner? Or was there more going on under the surface?

Did Aidan care about her more than he was willing to admit? The possibility gave her a tiny sliver of hope, but she didn't want to dwell on it too much. After all, a tiny sliver of hope could grow into a big fat obsession, right?

"And now you're starting to obsess about obsession." She sighed. Why couldn't she just be happy with things as they were? She could, by gosh, and right then and there, she resolved to do just that. Be happy. After all, she'd never had this much fun with a man before, never felt as sexy and attractive and radiant as she'd felt lately. She was startled to realize that she had a sensual nature, and it was Aidan who'd helped her see it. Now she wanted to fully embrace that part of her.

She closed up her house, changed into her pajamas and slipped under the sheets. She fell asleep and dreamed the same dream she'd been having for a few weeks now. She dreamed about her baby. But for the first time ever, Aidan was there in her dream, too, smiling as he held their child in his arms.

She moved to join her little family and both Aidan and the baby dissolved into mist, to be replaced by an image of her mother sobbing over the man who got away.

Ellie was jolted awake with tears in her eyes and a deep feeling of loss in her heart.

Eight

He didn't like to admit mistakes, Aidan thought as he jogged along the narrow peninsula of sand that separated the waters of Alleria Bay from the resort's marina. But now he had a feeling he'd made a big one.

The early morning breeze stirred the nearby sailboat riggings, causing them to bump up against the aluminum masts and ping in a sort of odd harmony. Usually Aidan enjoyed hearing the tinny, echoing sound on his early morning runs, but not today. He was too preoccupied with wondering whether he'd miscalculated or not.

He shouldn't have followed Ellie and watched her conversation with Blake. And when she walked away, he should've let her go instead of intercepting her. He should've kept his mouth shut and not said anything about Blake.

What if Aidan's interference drove her back to the other man? He couldn't believe she would go back to Blake, but it should certainly be her decision to make.

The sun hadn't yet risen over the horizon so the beach was nearly deserted except for a few hearty health nuts out for a pre-dawn swim in the bay. Aidan tried to concentrate on the rhythmic pounding of his feet on the soft white sand, tried to match it to the beating of his heart. But it was useless. He couldn't get the image of Ellie and Blake out of his head.

And why the hell had Blake come back *now?* Had he gotten word somehow that Aidan and Ellie were together? Not that they *were* together, not really. But since no one else but Logan knew about their pregnancy pact, it might look that way to outsiders.

"We're not a real couple..." Aidan heard Ellie's voice in his mind again and felt the same sharp stab of something....

He shook his head to push those thoughts out of his mind. Blake. The issue right now was Blake. Was Ellie contemplating getting back together with him? *We're not a real couple.* Damn it. Aidan had no real standing to make demands on her, so how could he insist that she stay away from Blake? Ellie had agreed that Blake was a jerk, but did she mean it? Or had she just said that to placate Aidan?

"Probably just said it to shut you up," he grumbled to himself.

Who could blame her?

She was right. They weren't really together. He had no claim on her. Damn it.

Fine. He'd made a mistake. But if he stepped aside, wouldn't Blake swoop in? Wouldn't that be a bigger mistake? Hell. He had to talk to Ellie again. Apologize. She wasn't pregnant yet, so if she wanted to renew her relationship with Blake, all Aidan could do was step aside. It was the right thing to do, even though Aidan would rather chew on glass than let her go.

Not that it mattered. If Ellie left him for Blake, Aidan

could find another woman in a heartbeat if he wanted to. But that wasn't the point.

"Yeah, what's the point, knucklehead?" he muttered, as he pounded down the beach.

The point was, he liked Ellie. A lot. More than any other woman he'd ever been with, if he was being honest. Not that it meant anything because Aidan had no intention of ever settling down with one woman. Even though his brother had finally met his match with Grace, it wouldn't happen to Aidan. He just wasn't the type to settle down.

Why would he? *Look around you,* he thought. He loved this place, loved the carefree lifestyle. Loved surfing, sailing, wheeling and dealing, beautiful women in bikinis bouncing around everywhere.

Yeah. The more, the merrier. It was way too easy to love 'em and leave 'em when plenty of beautiful women arrived on the island daily and only stayed for a week or two at the most. He called that a win-win.

On the other hand, if he were the type to settle down— which he wasn't—Ellie would be the perfect woman to settle down with.

But since he wasn't that type, he had to give Ellie the space she needed to make her own choices. If she would rather have Blake be the father of her baby, then…fine. Although it grated on Aidan. No, it more than grated. It infuriated him. It made him want to take his fist and shove it right in Blake's face.

He had a feeling that wouldn't make Ellie happy, but his own satisfaction quotient would be through the roof.

Aidan reached the end of the peninsula and stopped to breathe for a minute while enjoying the stunning view of clear blue water as far as the eye could see. He grabbed the small towel he'd tucked into his back pocket and used it to wipe the sweat from his forehead and neck. Then he pivoted in the sand and started the long run back to the hotel.

Hell, if Ellie wanted to go back to Blake, Aidan would have no choice but to let her go. And now that he was thinking about it, he had to admit that from one objective angle, it would be the best of all worlds. Ellie would have a father for her baby, someone she cared about (even though Aidan couldn't figure out why she would care about Blake), and she would stay on the island and raise her kid here and continue to work for Sutherland Corp. That was all Aidan had ever wanted in the first place. It was a win-win-win. Wasn't it?

Of course, there was still the irritating fact that Blake would end up as her baby's father, not Aidan. And that didn't work for him at all. That part was *not* a win. Aidan knew in his gut that he, Aidan, was the one who needed to be Ellie's baby's father. She couldn't trust Blake.

The man had already dumped her once. Who was to say he wouldn't do it again? And this time, he'd be walking out on a kid, much like Aidan's mother had done to him and Logan. No, Blake was absolutely the wrong choice for father material.

And hey, they had an agreement together. A binding legal document. So maybe it would be better if he stuck to the status quo and didn't say a word to Ellie. Why give her a chance to change things when everything was working so well for both of them?

"Hell." He tried to focus on something else, like the clean, briny smell of the fishing boats moored in the marina. The pungent scent reminded him of the first time he and Logan came to the island. They were on a fishing holiday and the bluefish they caught in Alleria Bay were the finest anywhere. They stayed a week longer than they'd planned and when they set sail for home, they were the new owners of the island.

Aidan slowed his pace as he approached the resort. He'd trusted in his luck back then, he reminded himself, and it had turned out well. He'd have to trust to his luck now, too. It wouldn't be easy, but he knew what he had to do. Ellie had to be the one to make the choice. And for Aidan, that meant standing aside to give her the room to do so.

He stopped abruptly at the water's edge. Something he'd refused to dwell on too heavily was the fact that Ellie hadn't gotten pregnant yet. Ellie hadn't brought it up and Aidan had simply figured they would continue having a good time until she announced she was pregnant. But now he wondered if maybe she was blaming him for not getting her pregnant immediately. Maybe she was ready to chuck Aidan and try this with someone new.

"That's ridiculous," he said aloud, immediately brushing that thought aside. Ellie wasn't the type of woman who would do something like that. But even if she was having second thoughts, Aidan refused to believe she would ever do anything so crazy as to choose Blake over him. Yet the fact remained that it was still her choice to make.

As he walked slowly across the white sand toward the terrace, Aidan reached an uncomfortable conclusion. He had started out wanting what was best for Ellie and the baby. Now he had to face the possibility that it might not be *him*.

"You want me to what?"

"I want you to go to Blake if you want to. It's your decision to make."

Ellie stared at him as if he'd just sprouted a second head. Maybe he had. He couldn't quite believe he was saying the words either. But they had to be said.

"It's my decision," she murmured.

"Yes. I shouldn't have followed you outside the other night," Aidan said solemnly. "It wasn't my place to interfere. Blake has offered you a choice and you need to do what's right for you."

Ellie searched his face for so long, he was about to start squirming. This wasn't easy for him, but it was the right thing to do.

Finally she said, "But you and I have an agreement."

"That's true," he said. "But you're running the show here, Ellie. I shouldn't have watched you and Blake when you were talking—it's just that that guy really bugs me and—never mind. Not the point. It was wrong of me to intrude. And if Blake cares about you…"

"You said he was a liar and a jerk," she reminded him. "Did you change your mind about him?"

"No, I didn't change my mind about him," Aidan said, resisting the urge to scowl. "I still don't like him. But this isn't about me. Look, I'm just afraid I might've pushed you into something you weren't ready for. So if you want to reconsider Blake, or any other guy, I need to give you the space to make a measured decision. It's your choice to make."

"I don't know what to say," she murmured, looking pensive.

He wanted to take her in his arms and kiss away every last ounce of doubt she'd ever had about herself. But he stayed on track and bit out the next words. "You have every right to go back to Blake if that's what you want."

"What do you want, Aidan?"

His jaw clenched and he pressed his lips together tightly, then forced himself to say the words. "I want you to do whatever will make you happy. You deserve to be happy, Ellie. And you deserve to make your own decision without me influencing you. More importantly, your baby deserves a father of your choosing."

And, damn it, she should choose him! But Aidan couldn't say that out loud.

She nodded slowly. "So you're saying you'd be fine if I decided that Blake or some other man would be a better choice to be the father of my child."

Hell, no! Was she going to make him say it out loud? Aidan wasn't sure he could. Finally he uttered the only thing left to say. "If that's what you want to do."

Ellie couldn't believe they were having this conversation. Her heart felt as if it were breaking in a thousand little bits. Did he really want her to choose Blake, or did he think he was being noble, offering her a choice? She had to remember that in the beginning, all Aidan had really wanted was to keep her on the island. If she went back to Blake, that goal would be achieved. As Aidan would say, it was a win-win.

Of course, there was no win for Ellie because apparently Aidan would be perfectly happy to see her go, and yet she would never return to Blake. She wasn't about to admit that to Aidan, though. Not now, with him so unwilling to take a stand either way.

Her head was spinning in confusion and pain. Could he really just let her go? She pressed a fist to her heart. Why did it have to hurt so much? She had tried so hard to avoid those pitfalls into which her mother had descended and now she herself was spiraling down into her own personal hell.

Right now there was only one thing she knew for sure. She needed to get away and think this through. She needed to stay away from Aidan and sadly, she couldn't do that if they were having sex together.

"What's going on, Ellie?" he said, a note of concern in his voice. "What are you thinking?"

She took a deep breath and gazed up at him. "I need some time to think, Aidan. I admit you've confused me. I need to stay away from you for a little while, just until I can put things into perspective."

His eyes narrowed on her. "Exactly what does that mean, Ellie?"

"It means we won't be having sex for a while."

"What?" he said. "Why the hell not?"

He looked so outraged that she squeezed his hand to comfort him. "I'm so sorry. I know our arrangement is strictly business, so maybe this is unfair of me to say. But I have to be honest with you. It's upsetting to hear that you don't have a problem with my going back to Blake. I thought we were having so much fun together, but now I see…well, I'm not sure of anything right now. Please just give me a little time to figure out what my next move will be."

"What if you find out you're pregnant?" Aidan said.

"Oh." She had to blink back a sudden wash of tears. She hadn't even taken that possibility into consideration. She took a few more deep breaths, then said, "I hadn't even thought about that. But if I find out I'm pregnant, there'll be no need to wonder who the father should be."

Ellie folded another crisp cloth napkin and added it to the pile. Ever since she was a young girl, whenever she needed to think about something important, she liked to do it while ironing. It was a mindless yet productive activity so she was able to accomplish something while doing almost nothing but allowing words and images to zip around in her head.

There was no way in the world she would ever start dating Blake again. Didn't Aidan know that? Of course he did. He was just feeling guilty about trying to influence her feelings about Blake.

But what annoyed the holy heck out of her wasn't the fact that Aidan had come to offer her a choice to go back to Blake or not. No, it was the fact that he didn't care one way or another what she chose to do! That's what bothered her most.

It hurt, frankly. She was bewildered and uncertain and just a little panicky about what to do next.

The smartest thing to do would be to avoid Aidan for the next two weeks, until she found out if she was pregnant or not. It wouldn't be easy because every time she saw him, all she wanted to do was kiss him and jump into bed with him. And that would be wrong. Although she couldn't quite remember why.

But at least she had told him the truth. At least he knew that he had upset her. The truth was important, she thought. But while she was telling Aidan the truth, maybe it was time for her to face the truth about herself. She was her mother's daughter. Was she turning into that woman? Ellie hated to think so, but she did seem to be wrapping herself up in Aidan's world more and more. And if that continued, she would eventually lose herself. And that frightened her more than anything else.

She stared at the stack of twenty neatly ironed napkins and the three smoothly folded tablecloths beside them. She wasn't nearly finished thinking about her problem and glanced around for something more to iron. Would it be too silly to iron her dish towels?

"Oh, no, you're not obsessed much," she muttered, and quickly put the iron and ironing board away.

He never should've said a damn word.

Knowing he'd upset Ellie was like having a drill pierce a hole through his gut. Over and over again. Her words played constantly in his head until he thought he would go crazy. He still couldn't believe that she'd apologized for being unfair to *him*. She'd tried to comfort him, for God's sake.

He thought he'd been doing the right thing for Ellie, but he was wrong. All he'd really wanted was for her to choose him over Blake. He'd wanted to hear her say the words. Like his own ego needed so much massaging? What the hell was wrong with him?

"Damn it," he muttered, as he slammed the tennis ball across the net. She was so sweet, he obviously didn't deserve her. But screw that. Even if she was too good for him, the bottom line was she was stuck with him. And let's face it, if she was too good for Aidan, then she was way too good for Blake. And that settled it. She wasn't going back to that worthless guy again. Not as long as Aidan had breath left in his body.

"Heads up, bro," Logan called from the other side of the net after the tennis ball whizzed right past Aidan's ear. "You're completely out of it today."

That was pretty much true, Aidan thought. The fact that he hadn't found Ellie in his bed that morning, for the first time in weeks, had rendered him almost useless today. He was going to have to do something about it, and soon. But he wasn't about to admit any of that to Logan.

"I can still beat you with one hand tied behind my back," he yelled. "Serve another one."

It was day seven without sex.

Aidan saw Ellie every day in the office, where she was the epitome of professionalism. She worked as hard as she ever had and was cordial and helpful at all times to Aidan and everyone else in the company.

It was driving Aidan insane. He had reached the end of his rope. Telling Ellie she was free to go back to Blake was surely the worst idea he had ever come up with.

Last night he'd actually gone into the bar to find a woman, any woman, to have no-strings-attached sex. He'd seen a few attractive women he knew would be willing to go for it, but every time he approached one of them, he changed his mind. They weren't that appealing, after all.

"What the hell is wrong with you?"

Aidan looked up and saw his brother standing in the doorway of his office. "Buzz off."

Logan ignored that and walked over to his desk. "Your temporary secretary is threatening to quit and Sarah from the mail room is in tears. What is your problem?"

"She forgot to sort my mail," Aidan griped.

Logan leaned closer. "I'm sorry, but I don't think I heard you right."

Aidan refused to repeat the idiotic complaint he'd just uttered. Instead, he grumbled, "You heard me."

"You're right, I did. And I'm wondering something."

"What?" Aidan glared up at him.

"Who the hell died and made you King?" Logan shouted in his face. "Sort your own damn mail!"

That's exactly what he was doing, but he wasn't about to admit it to Logan. "Thanks for your advice. Now you can leave."

"Not until you tell me what bug crawled up your ass and died." Logan began to pace back and forth in front of his desk. "You've been acting like a jackass for days now and everyone in the hotel is fed up with you. So pull yourself together. Either take a damn vacation, or get a hobby, or go get laid, but do something. Work it out, for God's sake."

"I can't get laid," Aidan muttered.

Logan stopped in his tracks. "Excuse me?"

"I said, get out of my office."

"No," Logan said slowly. "I think you said you can't get laid."

"Never mind what I said. I'm busy. Get out."

Logan grinned. "Is there a medical issue I should be concerned about?"

Aidan stood and pointed to the door. "Get. Out."

But Logan wasn't going anywhere and he had the nerve to laugh. "Oh, wait a minute. I know what this is about."

"You don't know jack, man."

"Yeah, this is about Ellie."

"It has nothing to do with Ellie."

"Really?" Logan thought for a second. "But when Grace talked to her, she said… Well, you probably don't care. Okay, I'll be going."

"Wait. What did Grace say? What did Ellie tell her?"

"Sorry. Gotta go."

"You're not going anywhere."

Logan snorted with laughter. "Oh, this is rich. You're in love with her."

"Get out."

"Okay, I'm going." He snickered and headed for the door. When he got there, he stopped and turned. "But do us all a favor and just admit it to yourself."

"There's not a damn thing I need to admit to anyone."

Logan held up his hands in surrender. "Fine, be miserable. Just stop taking it out on the staff."

Logan closed the door. Aidan sagged back in his chair and wondered what horrible sin he'd committed in a previous lifetime that had cursed him to be born a twin.

The following night, Aidan prepared to work later than usual on the contracts for another new restaurant in Tierra del Alleria, the island's only town. Tierra, as the locals called it, was a Victorian-era port town that overlooked a picturesque harbor that had grown in the last five years from a lazy fishing village to a hub for wealthy yacht owners, sports fishermen and the occasional small cruise ship. People came to experience the stunning views, laid-back charm, fabulous weather and world-class restaurants that lined the beach and pier.

The new restaurant owners planned to take advantage of the growing trend in gourmet artisanal vegetarian fare. Aidan figured the menu items would appeal especially to visiting celebrities and the wealthy wives of all those cigar-smoking yacht owners.

Thinking about the town reminded him of the dinner he'd shared there a few weeks ago with Ellie. They had snuck away from the hotel for the evening to wander and shop along the quaint waterfront. It was the most normal evening he'd spent in years, he thought. They had stopped for dinner at one of Aidan's favorite restaurants, a French bistro with phenomenal food and an excellent wine list. They were seated at the most prized table with a stunning view overlooking the scenic harbor and the sea of blue water that stretched on forever.

Ellie had ordered a rich cassoulet and Aidan the steak frites. The meat was tender and rare, the French fries deep fried to perfection. There was béarnaise sauce that Ellie had practically swooned over and each time she dipped a fry in the sauce and bit into it, Aidan felt himself grow more taut. They had rushed back home and made love for hours.

Damn it, where had that thought come from?

Aidan dragged himself back to the work before him, forcing himself to read through the various contracts for the new restaurant until he realized that one of the subcontractors' agreements was missing. He flipped through the file, but it wasn't there. Without much thought he buzzed Ellie, knowing she would be able to track it down for him.

A few minutes later, she walked into his office and his eyes drank in the sight of her. She wore a fire-engine-red dress with a short matching jacket and he wondered what the hell she was doing getting all dressed up like that.

As she approached the desk, he caught the scent of something irresistible. Was she wearing a new perfume? For some reason, that thought irritated him almost as much as the alluring blend of vanilla and citrus blossoms did.

He meant to thank her for bringing the contract by, but somehow the words came out differently. "What the hell did you say to Grace?"

She stopped and stared at him. "I beg your pardon?"

"You heard me," he said as he stood up and rounded the desk. "I don't want you talking to Grace without clearing it with me first."

"Really?" she said, tilting her head at him. "Is that some kind of new partnership rule? I'm not allowed to have a conversation with my girlfriends?"

That wasn't what he meant, was it? He scowled. "Not if it's about... Never mind. I just don't want you to—"

Her eyes narrowed and she stepped closer. "You don't want me to what?"

"Look, Ellie," he said, trying to sound reasonable. "It's none of my business if you and Blake..."

"What about me and Blake?" she said, her tone challenging.

He gritted his teeth and changed the subject. "Never mind. Just give me the file and go home."

"I'll give you the damn file." She slammed it down on his desk.

"Temper," he chided.

She pursed her lips and got right up in his face. "But who says I'm going home?"

A red haze of fury filled his vision at the thought of her going off to Blake's house.

"You're not going anywhere," he said, his voice low and threatening.

"Oh? And who's going to stop me?"

"Me." He grabbed her by her jacket lapels and yanked her against him and his mouth covered hers in an act of overt possession. She returned the favor with equal passion, her hips writhing against his already rock-hard erection as her lips searched his in a needy quest for more.

It was wonderful, Ellie thought, her mind drifting in a fog of sensual pleasure. Aidan was wild. Dangerous. Better than ever before. Or maybe it only seemed that way because it had been a lifetime since he'd kissed her.

Not that it meant anything. It was just sex. Wild, hot, fabulous sex, but still. It didn't mean anything more than that to Aidan. Or to her, she reminded herself. So even if he thought he could make demands on her, he still had no intention of ever settling down with one woman.

Ellie had been trying for seven long days to resist him, but she couldn't do it anymore. She knew she'd been obsessing over him, but she couldn't help herself. The good news was that she had finally recognized what her mom must have been going through all those years ago. It wasn't easy, but in her heart, Ellie had finally forgiven her. That was a big step.

And as for Ellie, she simply didn't want to deny her true self anymore. She resolved here and now to just enjoy what she and Aidan had for as long as she could. She was tired of obsessing about obsession. If fun was all Aidan was offering, then fun is what she wanted to have.

He grabbed her hair and pulled gently, wrenching their lips apart. "I mean it, Ellie. You're not going to see Blake."

She smiled. "Of course I'm not."

"Ever again," he warned.

"I already told him a week ago."

"Good. Come here," he muttered and kissed her again.

Two weeks later, the Duke cousins arrived on the island for the wedding of Tom Sutherland and Sally Duke.

Aidan and Logan greeted everyone as they climbed out of the limousine.

He gave Sally a hug. She stared up at him and pressed her hands to his cheeks. "Oh Aidan, I'm so happy you're my family."

The words struck him like a punch to the solar plexus.

"I'm happy, too," he managed, before Sally turned to Logan. Surreptitiously he blinked back a few drops of moisture that sprang to his eyes. Where the hell had that come from?

"Oh, look who's here," Sally cried, and rushed across the porte cochere.

Aidan turned in time to see her greet Ellie with a big hug and kisses on both cheeks. He frowned. How did those two know each other?

Logan elbowed him just then and chuckled. "Check it out. You are so dead."

Aidan was suddenly reminded of Sally's reputation as a matchmaker and was instantly suspicious. "How do they know each other?"

Logan shrugged. "They must've met on Sally's last trip here. Don't worry about it. I'm sure it's all friendly and harmless."

"Dude," Aidan said quietly. "On her last trip here, you accused her of being a witch."

"A *good* witch," Logan reminded him under his breath.

"Right, but still."

The last time Sally had visited Alleria, she'd spent a long time talking to Grace. Their cousin Brandon Duke had caught up with Aidan and advised him to warn his brother Logan that Sally liked to play matchmaker—and she played for keeps. She had uncanny luck in that area and the three Duke brothers were living proof. All three confirmed bachelors were now happily married with babies and the whole deal.

"You thought I was crazy for being concerned," Aidan said. "Remember?"

"Yeah, and I was right," Logan said. "You were crazy."

"I was just looking out for your best interests. And what good did it do? Look at you now. Happily married." His tone it was tinged with pity.

"True," Logan said cheerfully. "And now it looks like Sally and Ellie are new best friends. Hmm. Coincidence? I think not."

"Damn," Aidan muttered as he watched the two women chattering up a storm. "I'm gonna have to watch their every move now."

"Why bother?" Logan said, chuckling. "Just give in to the inevitable."

Aidan scowled. "You're doing it again."

"Doing what?"

"Wanting everyone else to get married just because you were dumb enough to get shackled."

"Yeah, that's me." Logan scratched his head. "What was I thinking? I like Ellie. Why would I want her to be stuck with you?"

"Very funny," Aidan said derisively.

"Dude, you just refuse to accept the fact that you're in love with Ellie."

"Oh, great," Aidan said. "One more delusional statement from the newly married man."

Logan slapped his back. "I'm gonna love watching you fall, bro."

Tom Sutherland and Sally Duke were married two days later surrounded by their closest friends and family. The setting was a secluded lagoon and waterfall nestled in the foothills of the rain forest with Alleria Bay as a backdrop.

Ellie was honored to be invited and was thrilled for Sally and Tom, who seemed so happy to have found each other after many years of living on their own. It was amazing to

Ellie that Sally, a widow who had spent so many years trying to track down her late husband's missing brother, Tom,
had finally found him.

With a soft sigh, Ellie thought that nobody deserved her
very own "happy ever after" more than Sally Duke.

"Everything is so beautiful," Grace whispered. "Thanks
for helping with the decorations."

"There wasn't much to do," Ellie said. "This setting is
perfect just as it is."

"It's my favorite spot on the island," Grace said shyly.

Ellie smiled. Her friend had confessed to finding the hid-
den lagoon while spore hunting one day and had returned
to enjoy it many times with Logan.

Ellie wished she could return here someday with Aidan.
It had to be the most romantic spot she'd ever seen. That
thought reminded her of Aidan and she glanced over at the
handsome twin brothers standing by their father's side.

As the ceremony began, Ellie paid special attention to the
vows the couple spoke. The words were so simple, yet filled
with so much emotion and love that Ellie was almost overwhelmed by everything she was feeling. As Grace passed
her a tissue, Ellie chocked it up to the simple fact that this
was a wedding, after all. She'd choked up during her sister's wedding, too. And Logan and Grace's nuptials had
been lovely, as well.

To keep herself from dissolving into tears, she stared
straight at Aidan, knowing his presence would help to
ground her. He looked so incredibly handsome standing
with Logan and Tom, surrounded by all that natural beauty.

At that moment, Aidan turned and winked at her. Ellie
smiled at him. And realized it didn't matter that someday
he might be the father of her child. Didn't matter that they'd
signed a legal agreement. Didn't matter that she seemed to
have succumbed completely to being her mother's daughter

when it came to obsessing over one man. Didn't matter that she'd never expected to fall in love and marry a man. The plain fact was that she loved Aidan Sutherland with all her heart and wanted to be with him for the rest of her life. Even if she was never lucky enough to have a baby, she would always want to be with Aidan.

And that was impossible.

All of a sudden, she couldn't breathe. She stood abruptly and stumbled to the aisle. Grace grabbed her hand and Ellie mumbled an apology as she left the ceremony. She made her way along the flower-petal-strewn path and staggered down the hill until she reached a bend in the trail. There she was able to sag against the trunk of a coco palm tree out of sight of the others.

"Oh, God. Oh, God." In a panic, she struggled to get enough breath into her lungs so she wouldn't pass out. Because she was suddenly struck by the immensity of her feelings. She was truly and irrevocably in love with the man.

Yes, yes, fine, she had always been attracted to Aidan. She'd always cared about him. But this was so much bigger than what she had felt before. Her heart ached with the enormity of it all. Did it show on her face? How could it not? There was no way she could return to the ceremony now.

"You fool," she whispered. She'd known all along that Aidan would never settle down with one woman. He clearly had some aversion to commitment that would never allow him to give himself to Ellie alone. Just look at the endless line of bikini-clad women he'd dated over the years. So now what?

"Ellie?"

She whirled around and saw Grace tiptoeing toward her. "Are you all right?"

Ellie gulped back tears. "You should go back to the ceremony, Grace. Logan will miss you."

"Logan's fine. I'm more worried about you."

Ellie shook her head, but didn't say anything.

"Oh, what's wrong, sweetie?"

"I can't talk about it," she whispered.

Grace sighed and took hold of Ellie's hand. "Weddings can be treacherous events, can't they? So unfair to us sensitive types."

"It's true," Ellie whispered.

Absently, Grace pushed an errant strand of Ellie's hair behind her ear. "Are you sure you don't want to talk about it?"

Ellie nodded.

"Is it Aidan?"

Ellie's eyes widened, but she clamped her mouth shut for fear that if she spoke one word, her eyes would let loose a flood of epic proportions.

"I know you love him," Grace said gently.

"Oh, God," she moaned. "You can tell?"

"Of course, sweetie," Grace said, nodding. "It's obvious to me how you feel, but apparently not to him. Men can be such dolts."

Ellie giggled. She wasn't prone to giggling, but she couldn't help it around Grace, who was such a brilliant scientist, but whose words were completely down to earth.

"Especially Sutherland men," Grace added. "They can be a real bummer to a girl's self-assurance. But who can blame us for falling for them? Let's face it, they're hot."

Ellie sighed. "I'll say."

"I'm just impressed that you were smart enough to recognize the signs for yourself." Grace shook her head in dismay. "I was totally clueless."

"But you're a genius," Ellie protested.

"Some genius," Grace scoffed, then smiled wickedly. "But I'm getting smarter every day."

"Then you must see how useless my feelings for Aidan are. He has no intention of ever settling down."

"No, of course he doesn't," Grace said seriously. "Never. Not Aidan. No way."

"You're not helping."

Grace laughed lightly. "Ellie, Aidan would have to be a complete fool not to fall in love with you. And my husband's twin brother is no fool."

Ellie smiled. "I appreciate you saying that, even if it's complete nonsense."

Grace laughed and rubbed her arm. "You look like you're feeling a little better. Can I coax you to come back to the wedding?"

"I guess so," Ellie said. "But will you promise not to tell anyone how stupid I was?"

"You're far from stupid, but if it makes you feel better, I promise. Now let's get back before the Sutherland men miss us too much."

Nine

She caught the bridal bouquet.

Aidan was standing on the sidelines drinking a beer with his brother and their Duke cousins as the ladies all gathered on the dance floor behind Sally. Without any warning, Sally heaved that big bundle of pink and white flowers and ribbons over her head, directly into the hands of Ellie, who had the good grace to look terrified by her good luck.

Sally turned and when she saw who'd caught the bouquet, she laughed. Clapping her hands happily, she called out, "I was aiming right for you, Ellie."

"What the hell?" Aidan muttered to no one in particular.

Earlier, during the hors d'oeuvres and champagne portion of the party, Aidan had caught Sally and Ellie deep in conversation again. He'd had a moment of concern but wouldn't have thought much more about it, except that Cameron had walked up at that exact moment.

"Listen, Aidan," Cameron had said, nudging his chin toward Sally and Ellie. "I've heard that you and Ellie have something going on, so I have to warn you. My mother has these weird special powers. You know that, right?"

"I've heard stories," Aidan said, not willing to agree and sound completely deranged.

Cameron shrugged. "Well, everything you've heard is true. So unless you and Ellie are planning to take your own trip down the aisle one of these days, I'd go over and nip that conversation in the bud."

Aidan frowned as Sally and Ellie laughed quietly together over something. Then he noticed that another few yards beyond the two women, his brother, Logan, stood with Adam and Brandon Duke. The three men were staring straight at him. When Aidan scowled, they all began to laugh uproariously.

He turned to Cameron, who had obviously been goaded into giving him grief. "Okay. Thanks for the warning, man, but I think I can handle it from here."

"Really?" Cameron said, raising one eyebrow. "Are you feeling lucky?"

So that had happened, and Aidan had quickly brushed it off as a practical joke played on him by his moronic twin. But then Sally had deliberately thrown her bridal bouquet straight at Ellie, who hadn't even lined up with the other ladies to catch it. What was that all about? Wasn't there some bizarre old omen that the woman catching the bridal bouquet would be the next to get married? He was going to have to look that up. Fast.

"Nice catch, champ," Logan said to Ellie, who laughed and grabbed him in a big hug.

The Dukes' wives all gathered around Ellie to congratulate her.

"Guess you're next," Trish teased.

Aidan felt a hard lump of something cold and near-panic-like settle in the pit of his stomach.

"I don't think so," Ellie said, but she blushed as she held the bouquet up to breathe in the floral scent. "I wasn't even trying to catch it."

"Then it's doubly meant to be," said Kelly, Brandon's wife.

Aidan frowned.

"Doesn't she look beautiful holding those flowers?" Sally said fondly.

Aidan jolted, then looked down, a little disturbed to see Sally standing next to him and staring directly up at him. He'd been so distracted by the flower toss that he'd let her sneak through his defenses.

He debated whether to call her out right then and there. Because really, this little matchmaking act of hers was beyond obvious, at least to anyone paying attention. Unfortunately, Ellie seemed to be the only one who wasn't paying attention.

A little desperate now, he glanced around. What about the Duke brothers? Was there no solidarity among males anymore? Where were his cousins and twin brother when he needed them? Instead of coming to his aid, they were all standing back enjoying the show. What the hell?

They'd all been innocent victims of Sally's relentless attempts to get them all married off. And she'd succeeded! Aidan was the last line of defense. The least they all could do was rally to his side when he needed them most. They were all brothers now. They needed to band together. But no. Looked like they were all anxious to see the last of them fall.

"Aidan, dear, are you all right?" Sally said with a concerned pat on his arm.

"Huh? What? Oh yeah, Sally. Fine," Aidan said, feeling like a cornered rat.

"Well, then?"

He had to mentally retrace their conversation. "Oh, yeah. Absolutely right. That was nice of you. Ellie looks great with the flowers."

"Yes, she does," the older woman said softly, tucking her arm through his. "Such a beautiful girl. You're so lucky to have her."

"As a business partner? That's for darn sure." That was all he was willing to say. Lucky? Damn straight he was lucky. He had thought he'd lost her to Blake, but now that he had her back, he wanted her for however long it lasted.

He followed Sally's gaze across the room and found Ellie. Sally was absolutely right. Ellie looked flat-out gorgeous today, flowers or no. She was wearing her hair up on top of her head in that sexy style he'd grown to like so much, if only because he couldn't wait to pull the pins out one by one and watch as each of her thick strands of hair draped gently across her shoulders. The pink roses she held in her hands looked perfect against her soft skin and rosy lips.

Still, Sally was up to no good.

The orchestra members came back from their break and began to play a slow, romantic love song. Several couples walked out onto the dance floor and began to sway to the melody.

"Oh, the music has started back up," Sally declared, and patted Aidan's arm once more. "I want to see all my sons dancing."

He had no argument with her there. Turning to her, he smiled and held out his hand. "May I have this dance, Mom?"

She let out a little gasp and Aidan had the distinct pleasure of watching her eyes well up with tears.

Two days later, the Dukes left the island and Ellie missed them horribly for an entire day. She loved having all those wonderful women around. They had included her in everything and it had turned into a sorority party. Or at least, it seemed like every sorority party Ellie had ever heard of or seen in the movies, since she'd never been involved in a sorority herself. The night before the wedding, Sally, Trish, Julia, Kelly, Grace, Ellie and Sally's two best friends, Beatrice and Marjorie, had stayed up late gossiping and laughing and sharing secrets and plans for the future.

"You'll come visit us in California," Sally had said, just before they'd all piled into two limousines to take them to the island's airport. She had gripped Ellie's hands and then hugged her so tightly that Ellie had felt tears prickling her eyes.

It wasn't an exaggeration for Ellie to feel that, for a few days, Sally Duke had been the mother she'd never had. She was warm and kind, older and wiser, a woman who loved unconditionally and would always be there for her children, no matter what. During their conversations, Sally had made her laugh and think and wonder and dream. Ellie hoped she could be that same sort of mother to her child someday, and she tucked Sally's California invitation away in a special place in her heart.

And now that things on the island had calmed down a bit, Ellie decided to follow Sally's advice. The older woman had made it sound so easy. Just tell him how you feel, Sally had said. Honesty was always the best way to go.

So with a deep, bracing breath, Ellie called up Aidan and invited him to her cottage that night for dinner. Tonight she would tell Aidan she loved him. Excited and more than a little bit nervous, she left the office early to set the scene for the most romantic evening ever.

Aidan set the phone down carefully and stared out the window.

"What's wrong?" Logan said, sitting across the desk from

him. "Who was that? You look like you just received a warning from the grave."

"Close enough," Aidan said numbly as his eyes narrowed in thought. "That was Ellie. She's invited me to her place for dinner tonight."

"Jeez, man, I thought something terrible happened."

"Maybe it did." His mind was racing, trying to stay a step or two ahead of the gorgeous woman who was taking up way too many of his thoughts lately. "Who knows what she has in mind?"

"Aw hell, you're right. This is despicable." Logan smirked. "A dinner invitation? Man, that's low. How could she do this to you? I hope you told her to take a hike."

Aidan made a rude gesture. "Go ahead and mock me, but this isn't funny. Ellie spent the last four days conspiring with Sally Duke at every opportunity. Now all of a sudden she wants to make dinner for me?"

"Oh man, that's sneaky," Logan said. "Yeah, you're right to be terrified—"

"Who says I'm terrified?"

"You should be. She could slip some aphrodisiac into the mix and turn you into her love slave."

Aidan tried not to dwell on the sudden image of Ellie carrying a satin whip and wearing a little black mask. And nothing else.

He gulped in air and pushed his chair back. "I'm finished talking to you."

Logan laughed. "You can't really be paranoid about this, can you? It's just dinner. And probably wild sex afterwards. Is that a problem?"

He frowned. "Maybe not."

"We've all been giving Sally too much credit," Logan said sensibly. "All we're really talking about is dinner and sex. End of story."

"It's not the end of the story." Aidan glared at his brother. "Are you blind? We have empirical evidence of Sally's power."

Logan was laughing so hard, he had to rest his elbows on his knees. "Oh man, I want to hear this."

Aidan held up his fingers and ticked off the evidence. "One, Sally talked to Grace. Two, you're now married to Grace. And *that's* the end of the story."

"My God," Logan said, feigning shock and dismay. "You're right."

"Thank you."

Logan grinned. "So what are you going to do about it?"

"I already told her I'd come for dinner."

"Call and cancel," Logan said easily.

Aidan frowned. "I don't want to do that. It would hurt her feelings."

"What do you care?" Logan asked. "You could be dodging a bullet here if she's truly plotting to get you to marry her."

"I know." Aidan thought about it and then sighed. "No, she's going to a lot of trouble to make a nice dinner. That's all this is. She doesn't want to get married. Hell, at first she was going to have a baby through a sperm bank so there's no way she's interested in getting married. It's ridiculous to worry about it."

"Then why are you worried about it?"

"I'm not," Aidan insisted. "We have an agreement. We even signed a *contract*. There's nothing else going on, so why am I letting Sally and all of you guys get to me? That ends here and now."

"Does it?"

Aidan blew out a breath of frustration. "I don't know."

Logan shot him a look of profound pity, then said, "Tell you what, bro. If it'll make you feel any better, I'm willing to work the Switch for you."

Aidan's eyebrows shot up at Logan's suggestion and he weighed the possibilities and drawbacks for a moment. The Switch was an old twin trick they'd used a few times in the past. As recently as a few months ago, they had pulled the Switch on Grace, but she had seen through the ruse within seconds and had laughed when Aidan tried to insist he was his brother.

As far as Aidan was concerned, that was as close to a declaration of love as you could get. After all, their own mother had never been able to tell the twins apart. Since then, they'd met no woman who could differentiate one twin from the other. Until Grace. That's when Aidan had realized that she was the perfect woman for his brother.

"Wait," Aidan said. "This won't work. She can already tell the difference between us. Remember that day in the office? You were sitting at my desk, but she knew it was you."

"That could've been a fluke," Logan said logically.

"I guess so."

The only thing Aidan knew for sure was that if he didn't take Logan up on his plan to do the Switch, his brother would issue a final decree to put up or shut up. So ultimately, Aidan's choice was a simple one.

"Fine," he said finally. "Let's do it."

"Cool," Logan said with a grin, as he rubbed his hands together. "Just don't tell Gracie. Now. What time is dinner?"

Ellie had just finished lighting the row of twinkling votive candles on the mantle when her doorbell rang. Thousands of butterflies in her stomach fluttered to life and she commanded them to calm down, but they just ignored her. Rubbing her tummy, she had to accept that she would always have this tingly fluttering reaction whenever Aidan came around.

She opened the door and smiled at him. "Hi."

"Hi." He extended a small bunch of pink and purple flowers toward her. "These are for you."

"Oh, how beautiful. Thank you." She took them and waved him inside. "Come in."

"Thanks."

Ellie started to ask Logan what he was doing here, but something made her hesitate. Aidan couldn't be sick or Logan would've said something right away. So what was wrong here? Maybe Aidan was on his way and Grace was planning to join them, too. That would be fun. Ellie had made enough pasta for ten people. But finally she decided to wait and hear what Logan had to say before she asked any questions.

"You look beautiful, Ellie," Logan murmured.

"Thank you. You look nice, too. Would you mind opening the champagne?" She pointed to the coffee table, where she had laid out a platter of appetizers, a bucket of champagne and two flutes.

"I'll be glad to," Logan said. He went through the motions, popped the cork off, filled the glasses, and handed her one. "What shall we drink to?"

Ellie smiled as she realized Logan wasn't going to say a word. They were teasing her! She wondered if Aidan was hiding out on the veranda, waiting to burst the door open and shout *surprise*.

"Let's drink to surprises," she said, and clicked her glass against his.

"To surprises." He took a sip, then set his glass down on the table. "Come here." He reached for Ellie and took her into his embrace. "Mmm, this feels good."

Ellie tried to sigh, but it was no use. She began to giggle. Her shoulders shook until she finally managed to push away from him—and laughed out loud.

"What is it, Ellie? What's wrong, honey?" He rubbed her back. "Please don't cry."

"Cry?" It took her a few more seconds before she could speak again. "I'm not crying."

"Then what are you doing?"

"That was my question," she said, shaking her head as her laughter subsided. "Logan, what're you doing here?"

"Logan?" he said indignantly. "I'm not Logan. I'm Aidan."

She rested her fists on her hips and shook her head. "Logan, does Grace know what you're up to?"

"Why would Grace care?" he said, trying to look outraged. "And stop calling me Logan."

"All right, fine. I'll stop." And suddenly she grabbed hold of his shirt and pulled him up against her. Staring into his eyes, she said, "Kiss me, please."

He gulped and said, "How about some more champagne, first?"

She let him go and smacked him on the arm. "Not before you tell me what's going on. Or would you rather I call Grace and ask her?"

"Damn it, Ellie," he said, shoving his hands in his pockets. "How the hell did you know it was me?"

"Is that some kind of joke? You guys may be twins, but it's easy to tell you apart."

"No, it isn't," he groused.

"Yes, it is," she argued. "I could tell you two apart from the first day I met you."

"How?" he demanded.

She was taken aback and reached for her champagne glass. After taking a sip, she said, "I'm not sure what to tell you. There are so many ways the two of you are different."

"No," Logan insisted. "There aren't."

Ellie chuckled. "Well, it's certainly true that both of you are incredibly handsome men."

"Yes, that's a given."

She laughed out loud. "Oh, Logan. What more is there to say?"

"Give it a shot," he said with an appealing grin.

This was the Logan she knew from the office, the man with whom she'd always enjoyed joking and sparring intellectually. Still, how could she possibly explain all the subtle differences she'd seen from the start between him and his brother?

She stared at Logan now and tried to pretend she was looking at Aidan. But it was impossible. They were virtually identical, from their haircuts down to their shoe size. They were both tall, both handsome, with the same shade of dark blond hair and dark blue eyes. But Aidan was more approachable, more touchable, more…lovable.

Although Grace would probably disagree with her, Ellie thought to herself.

"When Aidan smiles," she said finally, "his mouth curves up ever so slightly higher than yours."

"It does?"

"Yes, definitely," Ellie said with an emphatic nod. "And his eyes twinkle a bit more. Those are two differences I've noticed."

"Really?" Logan raised one eyebrow. "Did you ever consider the fact that his smile was a little brighter because of the way he feels about you?"

She paused to consider that. "No."

"Well, think about it."

As much as she wanted to, she brushed that improbable theory away instead and continued. "Aidan's wit is a bit sharper than yours."

"Sharper? Wait." He held up his hand. "I know you're not trying to say he's smarter than me."

"No," she said with a laugh. "But his sense of irony seems,

I don't know, more highly developed than yours." The fact was that Aidan made her smile, made her giggle and laugh, made her want to be a better person, made her want to spend her life with him. But she wasn't about to mention all that to his brother.

"So you're saying he makes you laugh?"

"Yes, that's it."

Logan smiled. "Again, this is your fault."

"My fault? How is it my fault?"

He shrugged. "You two travel so much together that you've developed an incredibly tight friendship. And that's totally cool. But it means that Aidan only shows his ironic side—and by *ironic,* I mean sarcastic and mocking—with the people he feels closest to. Like me. And you."

"But you and I travel together, too."

"Yes, but not as often."

"And you're also my friend, right?"

"I like to think so. But you and I don't seem to have the same sizzling chemistry between us that you have with my brother."

She felt herself beginning to blush. "Thank goodness, or Grace would take out a contract on me."

He chuckled softly, but it faded as a thought occurred to him. "Ellie, why aren't you attracted to me?"

She smiled. "You almost sound offended."

"I am," he said with mock sulkiness. "I'm just as cute as Aidan."

She laughed and patted his cheek. "Yes, you are. And Grace is a lucky woman."

"That's for sure," he said, grinning.

"And she's probably wondering where you are," Ellie added lightly.

"She knows I'm having dinner with you."

"Alone?"

His lips twisted. "Not exactly."

She checked her wristwatch. "If you hurry, you can still get back and have dinner together."

He gazed at her intently, as if to assure himself that she would be all right.

"I'll be fine," she promised, smiling confidently.

After a moment, he seemed to understand that she would be. "Okay, maybe I'll take off."

Her smile faded. Apparently, Aidan didn't plan on showing up tonight. She supposed she should've been flattered that the two men had gone to all this trouble to trick or tease her, but there was one question she wanted an answer to. She hated to ask, but she needed to know.

"Logan, can you tell me something before you go?" she said as she walked him to the door.

"Sure."

"Where is Aidan tonight? Is he out on a date with another woman?"

He whipped around. "What? Hell, no. Why would you think something like that?"

She bit her lip anxiously. "I just can't think of another explanation of why you'd show up instead of him. Maybe he met someone or…maybe he just got busy doing something else." She despised the helpless tone in her voice and shook herself out of it. "Oh, never mind. Forget I said anything. Have a good evening and say hello to Grace for me."

"Ellie, wait." He gripped her arm. "This was stupid. It was my idea. It's something we've done a few times before in the past and I thought it would be funny, but it's not."

"But Aidan went along with it."

He shrugged apologetically. "I didn't give him much choice."

"Why?"

"Look, Aidan cares about you a lot. And it scares him to death. When you called to invite him for dinner, he…"

She nodded slowly as she realized what he was inferring. "He thinks I'm pushing him into something."

"Yeah, and no matter what he says, he wants to go there. So do me a favor, okay?"

"What's that?"

Logan's smile was conspiratorial. "Keep pushing."

Ten

"She's in love with you."

"That's ridiculous," Aidan said, although the words caused a tug in his chest. With a sigh, he muted the basketball game he was watching. "Why are you even here? You should be having dinner with Ellie right now."

Logan grimaced. "Dude, she knew it was me the minute she opened the door. There wasn't much to say after that, so I made my excuses and left."

"You left her alone?" Somehow that bothered Aidan, knowing Ellie was all alone.

"Not the point," Logan snapped. "But yes, I left her alone. She wasn't in much of a mood for entertaining once she realized I wasn't you—and *you* weren't coming. She was hurt, and I don't feel real good about that. But my point is that she knew I wasn't you within seconds. The only other woman who's ever been able to tell us apart that quickly was Grace."

"I don't like where this is heading," Aidan groused.

"You're descending into Married Guy Hell again, aren't you?"

Frustrated, Logan paced back and forth in front of the television. He stopped abruptly and wagged his finger at Aidan. "Do you remember pulling the Switch on Grace? It wasn't that long ago."

"Sure," Aidan said casually, but began to frown as he remembered exactly what had happened. It had been his idea to pull the Switch on Grace because he had believed she was using Logan to further her career. And within seconds of the moment they met on the beach, Grace had recognized that he was Aidan and not Logan.

That was the first time Aidan had ever met a woman who could distinguish so easily between the two of them. And Aidan had realized after talking to her for those few minutes, that Grace was in love with his brother.

Funny how the world had now turned upside down and Logan and he had changed places.

It didn't matter. Logan might believe it, but it couldn't be true. Ellie didn't love him. She only wanted a baby, not a long-term relationship. Right? Nothing had changed, had it?

He cast a glance at Logan, who was still blocking the basketball game with his pacing. Aidan decided to strike a reasonable tone. "Ellie's known us a lot longer than Grace had, so it's natural that she would be able to differentiate between us."

"Not that fast. Besides, she said she's been able to tell us apart since the first day we all met in New York. We have different ways of smiling or something."

Aidan frowned thoughtfully. She'd always been able to tell them apart? "Get off it."

"Seriously, she described your smile. And your eyes." Logan accompanied his words with a gagging sound.

"Shut up," Aidan said mildly.

Logan held his hands up. "It's all true, bro. I was frankly sickened by the whole conversation, but this is what I do for you."

Aidan snorted a laugh, but he quickly sobered. "So you left her alone."

"Yeah, and now I'm gonna leave you alone and go home to my wife."

Ellie latched the front door and turned off the porch light. While she was disappointed and hurt that Aidan hadn't shown up for dinner, she also felt an odd surge of hope after talking to Logan. Maybe he was right and all Aidan needed was another push or two—or three—and he would fall neatly into her arms.

Ellie knew life couldn't be that simple, but after spending the last few days talking with Sally Duke, she had begun to realize that telling the truth was the most important thing she could do for herself.

And tonight, after talking to Logan and then, once he left, musing over their conversation and tying it in with Sally's words, Ellie experienced an amazing moment of insight. It had to do with her mother, of all things.

Ellie realized that it wasn't her mother's *obsession* that had destroyed her; it was the lies she'd told herself. Her mom had repeated the same lies over and over again, so often that she began to believe them. Her mother had spent her life lying to herself and that was her ultimate downfall.

As Ellie brushed her hair and removed her makeup, she was more determined than ever that if she wanted to be free of her mother's legacy once and for all, she had to tell Aidan the truth. Whether he wanted to hear it or not.

He'd hurt her. He didn't need his brother to tell him that. He knew Ellie. Now he stood at her door and wondered if she would even let him into her house. Would she listen to him? Hell, he didn't even know what to say to her besides begging her forgiveness.

Logan had said that Ellie loved him. That she'd always been able to tell them apart. So was Aidan coming to see her to hear her say those words?

Aidan shoved the panicky feelings to the back of his mind and knocked on her door. And waited.

When Ellie didn't come to the door immediately, he began to fear that she really wouldn't let him in. Well, she was going to have to let him inside because she loved him, damn it.

Finally she showed up, opening the door in her pajamas and bathrobe.

"Aidan, what are you doing here?"

"You invited me for dinner," he said in a rush.

"I did," she said calmly. "But when you didn't show up, I packaged it up and stuck it in the freezer." She seemed to debate whether to let him inside or not, but after a moment she opened the door wide. "Come in, Aidan."

Once inside, he pulled her into his arms and held her, stroking her hair and mumbling apologies. "I'm sorry. God, I'm an idiot."

She rubbed his back in reassuring strokes, comforting him more than he deserved.

Finally, he held her by the shoulders to meet her gaze. "My brother and I sometimes forget that we're not twelve years old. I apologize for playing that trick on you and for ruining the meal you prepared. I'd like to make it up to you by taking you to dinner tomorrow night."

She took a deep breath and said, "Dinner would be nice, thank you."

"What else can I do to prove how sorry I am?"

"Oh, Aidan, I know you're sorry," she said softly.

He kissed her tenderly. "I'd like to stay with you tonight."

"Why, Aidan?"

"Why?" He stared at her, stunned. "Because, you know, we're together. You like me. And I like you. And we...you know."

"You like me?"

"Of course I do, damn it." He scraped his hands through his hair in frustration because he knew he wasn't getting his point across. "You know that."

She took a deep, slow breath, then reached up and framed his face with her hands. "What I know is that I love you, Aidan. I know those words aren't what you want to hear, but it's how I feel. And after talking to Logan earlier, I realized that it was time for me to be completely honest with you. So if you still want to be with me after hearing that, then you're welcome to stay."

His gaze didn't quite meet hers as he wrapped his arms around her and buried his face in her hair. "I'd like to stay."

He hadn't returned the words and Ellie didn't expect him to. He'd apologized again for switching places with Logan and she had forgiven him again with a smile.

But she couldn't deny that her heart ached. She would live with the pain for now because she had no choice. But she had told him the truth and that helped. The simple fact was that she wanted to be with Aidan for as long as it lasted.

Logan had advised her to keep pushing Aidan, but she was hesitant to follow his counsel. After all, she could only push the man for so long with no results before her self-confidence crumbled. If that happened, she would lose everything.

So over the next two weeks, Ellie buried herself in her work. Call it self-preservation, but she avoided all but the most cursory business conversations with Aidan, even at night. They continued to spend their nights together and it was wonderful as always, but where they used to chat about anything under the sun, now Ellie did everything she could to keep the subjects centered on business, on the office, on work in general. Nothing personal. She had to do that. To protect herself more than anything else.

Ellie had already confessed her love. Aidan knew how she felt so there was really no point in saying so over and over again. Besides, if she did, if she allowed herself to indulge in loving him openly, she would get caught up in pretending that they might actually have a life together and forget that the only thing they had between them was a thin, legal document. They didn't have love. Didn't have a future. All they had was a rather elusive goal to get her pregnant. Once they achieved that, Ellie had no doubt that Aidan would begin to make excuses to stay away from her. Eventually she wouldn't see him at all except at work or when he and his family wanted to visit with their baby.

And if that wasn't the most depressing thing in the world, she had also begun to notice that Aidan seemed perfectly willing to give her all the space she wanted, thus confirming in her mind that she was indeed losing him. But that was impossible, she chided herself. How could she lose him when she'd never really had him to begin with?

Aidan brought the small fishing boat to a stop in a secluded bay on the other side of the island from the resort. As he set up the deck chairs and grabbed the fishing poles, Logan pulled two bottles of beer from the ice chest, popped them open and handed one to his brother.

Aidan took a long slug, then set the beer bottle into the built-in drink holder on the arm of his chair. He baited his hook, then cast it into the water.

"Perfect day," he said, relaxing in his deck chair.

"Yeah, beautiful." Logan joined him and readied his fishing rod. "I love this spot."

"Yeah, me too."

"Best decision we ever made was to buy this island."

"I'm with you there."

They continued to fish in blessed silence for three and a half minutes or so, until Aidan blurted, "She's driving me crazy."

Logan laughed out loud. "I should've taken bets on how long you could last without bringing up the subject of Ellie."

"It's not funny," Aidan grumbled. "She won't stop working."

"I'll just mention this in case it hasn't crossed your mind," Logan said. "But Ellie is our partner now. When she works hard, we make money. See how that works out? It's a good thing. A win-win."

"I'm clear on the concept," Aidan said drily. "I'm just a little worried about her, that's all. Lately she's completely obsessed with work. Eats, sleeps and breathes it. It's all she talks about. Even when I try to change the subject to something else she's interested in, like books or movies, she winds the conversation right back to the office."

"Must make for some stimulating pillow talk."

"Shut up."

"Wait. Are you two still…you know?" Logan made a tangled gesture with his fingers.

"Shut up," Aidan repeated more forcefully.

"Is that a no?"

"No, it's not," Aidan said. "We're doing just fine in that department, thank you for your interest."

"Just trying to get the full picture."

Aidan scowled. "But even at night lately, Ellie doesn't say much unless it's work related."

"Might be a defense mechanism," Logan said as he adjusted the rim of his ball cap to better shield his eyes from the sun.

"What the hell's that supposed to mean?"

Logan's line tugged and he moved quickly to test it. "False alarm," he muttered, sitting back in his chair. "Okay, so you've got to look at this whole situation from her point of view. It's not like you've vowed eternal love to her, so she's starting to face facts. You're only sticking around to get her pregnant. Once that happens, you're gone. So even though she's in love with you, she doesn't see a future with you." He shrugged. "And so she's starting to pull back emotionally."

Aidan scowled at him. "Thank you, Dr. Freud."

"Hey, you asked. And please, you don't have to be a psychiatrist to see it. Just not blind…like some people."

"I'm not blind. I'm…focused."

"On all the wrong things."

"This is your fault," Aidan blurted.

"How do you figure that?" Logan sounded outraged.

Aidan eyed him suspiciously. "Now that I think about it, she started changing right after you pulled the Switch."

"Don't go blaming this on me," Logan said, laughing as he took another sip of beer. "If you'll recall, you began pulling away from her at Dad's wedding. That's when you started getting paranoid because of Sally."

"No, I didn't." But as he thought back, Aidan realized he'd forgotten how much he'd mistrusted his new mom. He would have to call her one of these days and tell her he was sorry about that.

He reeled in his line and re-baited his hook, then tossed it back into the water. And thought about Ellie.

She loved him.

She'd told him right to his face and he hadn't said a word back. But what could he say? He was crazy about her, but that was hardly love. Now that he thought about it, he wasn't even sure what love was. He just knew he wanted to be with Ellie all the time. Was that love? Hell, he was going to go crazy over that stupid question, and his brother wasn't helping.

"You're not helping," Aidan muttered aloud.

"You talking to me?"

"Never mind."

"I'm worried about you, bro," Logan said, but he was grinning like an idiot and didn't look worried at all.

Aidan shook his head in disgust. He grabbed his beer bottle and downed the rest of it. He would never truly understand women or love or anything related to those two subjects and it was useless to start trying now.

Suddenly a hefty fish yanked at his line and he pulled back and began to reel it in. He and his brother grinned at each other.

Fishing, he thought as he fought with the line. He understood fishing. Trying to figure anything else out only led to madness.

Two days later, Ellie stared in astonishment as a little pink cross appeared in the screen of the testing stick.

"Oh, my," she whispered. No wonder she'd been so ridiculously emotional lately. Was it any surprise that she'd been behaving like a nutcase, drowning herself in work until she couldn't see straight? She'd been a maniac for weeks now. And no wonder.

"I'm pregnant!" she exclaimed. She rose from the chair and twirled around her kitchen. She could feel her heart thumping wildly in her chest. "Wait 'til I tell Aidan. He's going to be so…"

She stopped, inhaled and exhaled a few times to catch her breath, and wondered. Aidan was going to be…what? Thrilled? Blissful? Indifferent?

"Thrilled, definitely," she said firmly, and danced around again. But her steps faltered immediately. She was going to be a mother, so now wasn't the time to dwell on foolish dreams of a family that included Aidan. Yes, he had insisted on supporting her and the baby. He'd written it into the contract. But that didn't mean he would be falling in love, moving in and starting a life together.

But that wasn't fair, she told herself. Of course Aidan would be thrilled about the baby. He was a good man and he cared about her a lot, she knew he did. He just didn't love her.

Or maybe he did love her, as Logan seemed to have indicated the night he came to her house. He seemed to believe that Aidan simply wasn't willing or able to say the words or act on his feelings. And that was fine, she thought resolutely, trying to convince herself of the lie.

"So much for telling the truth," she muttered, then quickly shook away the words. This wasn't the time to be thinking unhappy thoughts. She was pregnant and happy about it. This is what she'd wanted for so long; a man had never been a part of the equation.

But oh, now she wanted a man to be a part of her life. One man in particular. She couldn't imagine living without Aidan's warm arms around her and his ruggedly beautiful body snuggled up to hers. The thought of his skin rubbing up against hers, his amazing hands, and mouth and… Hmm.

There was a time when Ellie would've been embarrassed by her sexy thoughts, but not anymore. She had discovered the sensual side of herself, thanks to Aidan. And she wasn't ready to deny that part of her life, even with a child on the way. In fact, she was anxious to explore that side of herself even more now, and she wanted to do it with Aidan.

She wrapped her arms around her stomach and said a little prayer of thanks and hope that she and the little life growing inside her would be healthy and together they would make a happy little family some day soon.

But more than anything else, she hoped that Aidan would open his eyes and realize that this was right where he belonged.

With resolve, she left her house and crossed the coco palm grove to find Aidan and share the news. As she rounded the terrace, she saw Aidan walking toward a table of guests. Her heart gave a little jolt at the sight of him looking so handsome in a crisp white shirt tucked into beige linen trousers. So simple, yet so swoon-worthy, she thought with a smile.

She raised her arm to wave at him, but just then, one of the women jumped up from the table and wrapped her arms around his neck. Her curvaceous bikini-clad bottom barely covered her butt as she wiggled against him.

Ellie could hear the woman's shrieks of excitement all the way across the expansive terrace.

"Squeee! Aidan! Squeee!"

Those probably weren't her exact words, but it was something along those lines. The three women seated at the table chattered loud enough for Ellie to hear that the woman hugging Aidan had been here before and had been telling them about the hot guy who owned the resort.

Well, she was right about that. He was hot.

Ellie's vision blurred. Had Squeee Woman been with Aidan before? Had she been one of his bikini babes?

Without another clear thought, Ellie spun around and headed back to her cottage.

She felt faintly nauseated and it had nothing to do with being pregnant. No, this feeling had everything to do with her being dumb enough to fall in love with a man who had only been trying to finagle a way to keep her working on the island and give her child two caring parents instead of just one. To accomplish that, he had offered her a baby and the partnership she had always wanted.

As she walked through the palm grove, she conceded that she should be grateful. After all, Aidan had lived up to his part of their bargain. She couldn't fault him for that. Ellie had the partnership she had always wanted, and more importantly, she would soon have the baby she'd always dreamed of. Their bargain had been met. Now Aidan could return to his carefree, commitment-free lifestyle.

The only question in Ellie's mind now was, how could she continue to live here and work with Aidan, knowing she was in love with him and knowing he didn't love her back?

She had really thought she could do it, but just now, seeing that woman throw herself at Aidan, had changed her mind in an instant. She simply couldn't imagine herself caring for a newborn baby while Aidan went back to flirting with the bikini babes. That woman snuggling up to him just now had brought that painful fact into clear focus.

But that didn't mean she would run off like a coward with her tail between her legs. Ellie wasn't that person. There was no way she would quit her beloved job. She had signed a partnership contract. She was a full junior partner in Sutherland Corporation. She was a damned fine businesswoman and she would never walk away from that. And she refused to give up her wonderful life and all her good friends on the island. She loved it here. So no, leaving was absolutely not an option.

Besides, Ellie would never deny her child a fulfilling relationship with its father, even if Aidan refused to have anything to do with the baby—which he wouldn't do, she hastened to add. He wasn't that kind of man. Even though he had vowed never to get married, he was too good a person to turn his back on any child he'd fathered.

So she was in a quandary. There was no question about whether she would stay on the island or not. She was staying. But she could no longer live here at the resort, not with Aidan so close yet so unavailable. And that was another painful realization, because she loved her little cottage on the resort grounds. She wondered absently if she would be able to find a small house on the south shore. Or maybe something closer to town. It was only a short drive away.

"Oh, God." It was all too confusing to sort out right away. And it was downright heartbreaking, if she was being honest.

What she needed to do right now was go somewhere, get away and think. Somewhere quiet. Somewhere off the island so she wouldn't be tempted to run to Aidan and beg him to take her in his arms, touch her, love her. Which she would never do, for goodness sake.

Don't even think about doing something so beyond idiotic, she scolded herself. She would never try and cling to a man who didn't love her. That was exactly what her mother had done and look where it had gotten her. Ellie would never do to her own child what her mother had done to Ellie and Brenna.

With resolve, she ran into her house and pulled her overnight bag down from the closet. She tossed several casual outfits into it, added some underwear and toiletries, a few books and a pair of pajamas. She zipped the bag shut and went out to the kitchen to make four quick phone calls.

After that, she sent Aidan a quick text message to let him know she had to leave the island for a few days. An emergency, she said. But this time, she would be gone before he could do anything about it.

She grabbed her bag and locked up her house, then headed for the hotel. She detoured through the kitchen to avoid seeing Aidan with his guests on the terrace. Serena stood at a counter writing notes, but looked up from her clipboard to greet her. "Hey, you. Don't forget girls' night next Thursday."

"I won't," Ellie assured her. As she crossed the lobby,

the assistant concierge said hello and two of the bartenders shouted her name. She smiled and waved to all of them but kept walking toward the hotel entry to meet the limo driver she'd called.

She called out a greeting to Marianne as they passed each other. That's when Ellie slowed her pace a little as she realized that here was one more thing to cheer about. Ellie was no longer the overachieving, anchorless girl she'd been as a teenager . She had a home here on Alleria, and she had a life, and friends, and she was a normal, healthy woman with a heart filled to the brim with love to share with the right man. And she deserved that man to love her back equally. And soon she would have a baby, and her child deserved all of those things, too.

And she was no longer willing to settle for less.

"Ellie!"

Ellie turned and saw Grace jogging toward her, just as her limousine pulled up.

"Hi, I saw you from the lobby and I…" Grace noticed her suitcase. "Are you going somewhere?"

The driver stepped out of the car and took her bag.

"I'm going to visit my sister for a couple of days."

Grace gave her a hug. "I'll miss you."

Ellie felt her throat close up.

Grace frowned. "Is everything all right?"

"Yes. No. Yes. Oh, God." Ellie burst into tears.

"Oh, honey." Grace pulled her into her arms and hugged her. "What did Aidan do to hurt you?"

"Aidan? No. Nothing. He's happy. I'm fine." Ellie hiccupped and quickly dried her tears. "This is silly," she muttered and straightened her shoulders in an attempt to be an adult about things. "Good heavens, I'll only be gone for a few days, but saying goodbye always chokes me up a little. Like weddings. Pay no attention to me."

"They do that to me, too," Grace said, nodding in sympathy.

Ellie knew she hadn't tricked Grace, but her friend was sweet to give her a pass.

"Please call me if you want to talk," Grace added. "And hurry back. You know everyone here loves you, Ellie."

"I do." She sniffed, in danger of spilling more tears but determined not to. "Thank you, Grace. I'm so lucky to have you for my friend."

"I'm the lucky one, Ellie. I need all the friends I can get." She squeezed Ellie's arm. "And so does Aidan. Believe me, he needs you more than you'll ever know."

"We'll see," she said, and pasted a cheery smile on her face. She had a feeling she looked demented, but smiling was the only thing she could think to do to stop the onslaught of more wretched tears. "I'd better go now. I have to make my plane."

"Bye, Ellie," Grace said softly. "See you soon."

"What do you mean, she's gone? Where the hell is she?"

"I'm sorry, Mr. Sutherland," Ellie's efficient secretary said. "All she said was that she had to leave the island for a few days."

Aidan stormed out of Ellie's office suite and returned to his own. Where the hell had she disappeared to? What "emergency" did she have to run off to?

He'd seen her dashing away from the terrace over an hour ago and would've gone after her, but he'd been waylaid by some returning guests who'd insisted on talking his ear off.

Not that he would ever complain about the resort's guests since they provided a portion of the hefty income that kept Sutherland Corporation in business. But frankly, he'd had his fill of all those overly made-up, bikini-clad socialites whose only job was to spend money jetting from one destination point to the next, according to the season.

And another thing. He didn't understand any woman who piled on makeup and perfume just to sit and sweat by a pool in the tropics, but that was a question for another day.

He knew Ellie had seen him on the terrace, but she hadn't stopped and waited for him. He'd figured she was in a hurry to get somewhere and he would find her later. The minute he'd seen her on the terrace, he'd concocted a plan to whisk her away to the rain forest for a sultry afternoon of lovemaking under the waterfall. He missed having her in his arms.

But when he'd gotten back to his office, he'd found her text message saying she was leaving the island. That's what he got for forgetting his phone in the office. That was another thing he blamed entirely on Ellie. He'd been so discombobulated by her behavior lately that he was forgetting to tie his own shoelaces. Yesterday, he'd almost missed their weekly conference call with the New York investors. Logan had been forced to send out a search party for him.

"Not important right now," he muttered. He needed to figure out where Ellie had gone and go after her. He tried calling her cell phone, but she didn't answer. Where in hell had she gone?

"I hope you're happy."

He turned and saw Grace standing at his doorway. "Why? What do you know?"

"I just know that Ellie is the best thing that ever happened to you and you're going to lose her."

"No, I'm not," he said a bit desperately. "You know where she's gone. Tell me so I can go after her."

"Why?"

Aidan stared at her, wondering if Grace was losing her grip on reality.

"What do you mean, why? Because I need her here, that's why."

"Yes, but why do you need her?" Grace folded her arms over her chest, tipped her head to one side and narrowed her gaze on him. "Did she forget to sign an important contract? Did she neglect to make a phone call to a new client?"

Logan walked up and stood behind Grace. Aidan glared at his brother, but Logan just smiled and wrapped his arm around Grace.

"I don't have time for this," Aidan said. He checked his phone for the tenth time in two minutes, but there were no new messages from Ellie.

With an abrupt huff of frustration, Grace stomped her foot. "Aidan, why do you want to go after Ellie?"

"Yeah, bro," Logan drawled. "There's nothing too pressing going on right now. Let her take a few days off."

"No. I need her here."

"Why?" Logan asked.

He needed her. Wasn't that enough? "Okay, both of you, get out."

Grace shook her head. "You're such a knucklehead."

Aidan raised an eyebrow at that, then glanced at his brother. "Does she call you names like that?"

"Not so much anymore," he said.

"Great. So it's just me."

Logan walked over to the bar and poured two shots of scotch. He handed one to Aidan, who scowled, but took the glass and downed it.

"Thanks, I needed that," Aidan said. "Now you can go."

"I don't think so," Grace said.

"Nope, we're just getting started." Logan sat down in the visitor's chair and pulled Grace onto his lap.

"This should be good," Aidan muttered, and had no choice but to sit back down at his desk.

"I don't care if you're too stupid to admit you're in love with the woman," Logan said. "What I do care about is that we might've just lost the best business partner we'll ever have because you're too boneheaded to admit it."

"Something happened to make Ellie leave," Grace said. "What did you do?"

"I didn't do anything. I was on my way to take her up to the lagoon for the day."

"Oh, that's so romantic," Grace said, and smiled at Logan. But then she turned and frowned at Aidan. "So why did she run off?"

Aidan thought about seeing Ellie across the terrace. She'd looked right at him, then turned and left. Why? Then it hit him.

"Damn it," he muttered. "There were some guests flirting with me. It didn't mean anything, but that's the moment Ellie…"

"But Ellie's not the jealous type," Logan said. "It must've been something you said."

"She's not the jealous type, but she does have a gentle heart," Grace said. "And she's pretty certain you're not willing to give her yours. Seeing you with those women might've brought that hard lesson home to her."

Aidan brushed his hand through his hair in frustration. Grace's words made sense, even if he hated hearing them.

"Why are you keeping Ellie at arm's length?" Logan asked quietly. "Why won't you just admit that you love her as much as she loves you? You can trust her, Aidan. She won't hurt you."

Aidan sneered at his brother. "Look who's Mr. Relationship Expert."

Logan laughed. "Turnabout is fair play, dude. Remember a while back when you played the expert?"

Aidan nodded. "Yeah, back when you played the idiot."

Logan chuckled. Gazing at his wife, he stroked her hair. "Yeah. That was me."

Unable to watch the two lovebirds any longer, Aidan got up and poured himself another shot of scotch. He stared at the glass, then glanced out the window at the incredible view of palm trees swaying along the white sand beach with the azure waters of Alleria Bay in the distance. It was one more symbol of what they'd strived to accomplish throughout their lives. This piece of land should've meant everything to him. But right now, it didn't mean much because Ellie wasn't here with him. Was that the real reason why he'd tried to keep her on the island in the first place? Damn. It had nothing to do with keeping the business going. It had to do with keeping Ellie near him. Everything was better when she was by his side. In business, in pleasure, on the island, flying off to New York. Everything worked when Ellie was with him.

God, she'd only been gone an hour or so and he missed her. Where was she? He needed her here. On the island. With him. This island, this symbol of accomplishment, meant nothing if he couldn't share it with the one person he'd grown to love more than anything else in the world.

"So what's your plan, man?" Logan asked him.

Aidan gritted his teeth, knowing there was only one thing to do. He drained the shot glass and slammed it down on the counter, then turned and faced his brother and Grace. "My plan is to grovel as much as it takes to get her back."

"But why, Aidan?" Grace asked softly.

Aidan smiled as he realized that Ellie had asked him the same question that night he and Logan had pulled the Switch. He had rushed to her house to see her and had wanted to spend the night with her and all she had said was, *Why?*

He turned to his brother and Grace. "Because I love her."

"Good answer," Logan said. "Just might work."

* * *

Ellie had just settled on the couch and was about ready to doze off when the doorbell rang. For a moment, her shoulders tightened at the thought of Aidan coming for her. But he didn't even know where she was! It was just one more example of her crazy obsession with the man.

Besides, it was mid-morning in Atlanta, not Alleria. Aidan was a thousand miles away. Brenna had rushed out to the market while the kids were in preschool. Her husband, Brian, was at work. And Ellie was already tired, so she decided to ignore the doorbell.

When the doorbell rang again, Ellie grumbled. It was probably someone Brenna knew, so she really should answer the door. When it rang yet again, it was clear that the person wasn't going to go away.

"Hold your horses," she muttered as she stood and walked to the door. She pulled it open and blinked, not quite trusting her eyesight. Had she conjured him up by magic? Did he have to look so wonderful that he made her mouth water? She wanted him so badly, she could feel her knees weakening.

"Aidan."

Without waiting for an invitation, he walked right into the house, shoved the door closed, pulled her into his arms and kissed her.

She savored his presence, the brush of his clothing against hers, his scent, the taste of him on her lips, and wished the moment would last forever. But it couldn't, of course.

"I know you're in love with me, Ellie," he said immediately after the kiss ended. "I'm taking you home."

"I'm in love with you?" she said. "Is that all you came here to tell me? Go home, Aidan."

"Don't deny it," he said. "You love me."

She stomped away from him, then whipped around. "Why would I deny it? I've already told you I'm in love with you.

It's no big revelation. But if you think I'm going to drop everything and go back with you to Alleria, you're wrong."

"We need you, Ellie."

"We?" she said, a little too loudly.

He sighed heavily. "All right. I need you. Okay? I can't seem to do anything without you."

"Oh, right, you need me," she said in a withering tone. "You don't look too happy about it."

"I'm happy," he said loudly.

"Just admit it, Aidan. You'll say any outlandish thing you can think of to get me to come back to work."

"I don't care if you come back to work," he retorted. "You can quit your job for all I care. I just want you to come back to me. I need you in my life."

"But you have so many other women who want you." Oh, no, she thought. Why did she say that? She sounded like a jealous harpy.

And he knew it. Which was why he was grinning broadly now. "I knew you saw me on the terrace. Why didn't you rescue me from that horrible woman? She ambushed me."

"Oh, please," she muttered. "You poor baby."

"It's true," he said, biting back a smile. "Besides, I was on my way to find you so we could sneak off to the waterfall and make love all afternoon."

She almost sighed at the thought of them lazing away the day in the rain forest. She wanted him so much, it was killing her.

"But you ran away," he said, brooding. "I couldn't find you anywhere. Why?"

She wanted to tell him why, wanted to throw herself into his arms and beg him to love her. Instead, she asked, "What are you doing here, Aidan?"

He gazed at her musingly. "I was an idiot not to realize

years ago how amazing you are. I've wanted you all this time."

She blinked. "What? Why didn't you say something?"

"Did you hear the part about my being an idiot?"

She blurted out a laugh. "It's my favorite thing you've said so far."

"It's true, Ellie. I've been so stupid. It took your leaving to make me realize how much time I've lost, but I'll make it up to you, I promise." He held her shoulders and gazed into her eyes. "I love you, Ellie. I love everything about you."

"Y-you love me?"

"I do. I even love your slide presentations and your sensible pantsuits and the way you shove your pencil behind your ear when you're concentrating on your notes."

"Oh, good grief, Aidan," she said, covering her face with both hands. "I sound like a schoolmarm."

"I love schoolmarms," he said, pulling her hands away and kissing them, one finger at a time. "And pantsuits." After a moment, he met her gaze again. "But if it's not too sexist, can I admit I prefer your little bikini most of all?"

"Of course you do," she said drily.

"I cannot tell a lie." He smiled, and one corner of his mouth curved even higher than the other, just as Ellie had explained to Logan. His grin widened and his eyes twinkled and she fell in love with him all over again.

"Oh, Aidan," she whispered.

He smoothed her hair back from her face. "Please come home. I promise you're the only bikini babe I've ever loved. Please, Ellie. I miss you in my bed, but most of all, I miss you in my life."

She took a breath and let it out. "I miss you, too."

"Come home, then," he said, squeezing her hands in a sensual plea. "Come home and start a family with me. We can tear up the custody agreement because I want a big family with lots of babies. I promise they'll always know how much I love them and their beautiful mother. Please come back to the island, back to our home. Marry me and love me always, Ellie."

How could she say anything but yes? "I love you so much, Aidan. Of course I'll come home with you and marry you."

"Thank you," he whispered. He kissed her again and she could feel the promise in his touch.

When he opened his eyes and gazed at her again, she smiled shyly. "I'm glad to hear you say you want babies, because I'm pregnant, Aidan."

His eyes widened and he gazed down at her. "Oh, my God. Is it true?"

She took his hand and pressed it lightly against her stomach. "Do you mind?"

"Mind?" he said, and then laughed. "No. I think I'm speechless. But very, very happy." And he kissed her again.

Ellie couldn't believe her heart could be so filled with love without bursting.

When she opened her eyes, Aidan was staring intently at her. "I can't wait to get home," he murmured. "I want to make love with you all night long. And I still intend to take a day very soon and go up to the waterfall where I plan to explore every beautiful inch of you."

Ellie shivered with need. That tingling feeling she always felt around him was back and she couldn't wait to show him how much she loved him. Every day for the rest of their lives together. With a smile, she took hold of his hand. "Take me home, Aidan. Take me back to Alleria where we both belong."

Epilogue

Three years later

"Twins?" Logan exclaimed. "Are you kidding?"

Ellie rubbed the slight bump of her tummy, then smiled up at Aidan as his hand covered hers.

"That's what the doctor says," Aidan explained to his brother as they relaxed under the pergola overlooking the secluded cove. They were surrounded by their large, extended family and Aidan couldn't help smiling as he watched his two-year-old son, Bobby, stretch to plant his sandy feet in his older cousin Jake's footsteps.

There were kids everywhere. The Duke and Sutherland families had established a new tradition of spending the holidays together at the charming boutique hotel the Duke brothers had built on the northern coast of Alleria. The hotel had been built into the side of a cliff and overlooked one of Alleria's beautiful views. Flowering vines cascaded down the hillside and the pristine white sand beach was dotted with colorful umbrellas. Sailboats bobbed in the azure waters beyond the breakwater.

Logan and Grace were here with their eighteen-month-old twin girls, Rosie and Lily, and the three Duke cousins had brought their entire brood. As far as Aidan was concerned, there was nothing better than Christmas in the tropics, and he was looking forward to a rollicking Christmas dinner with the whole gang later that afternoon.

His dad and Sally had made the trip, too, of course. Sally had made it a habit to keep in close touch with Aidan and Logan and considered them to be her boys along with her three Duke sons.

Aidan watched Sally laugh at something one of her grandchildren said. He rubbed at the twinge in his chest as he recalled the exact moment when he had realized that Sally had become the mother of his heart.

"Twins run in the family," his dad, Tom, said, smiling fondly at Ellie.

"They must," Logan said with a laugh.

First there had been Aidan and Logan, then Logan and Grace gave birth to twin daughters, and now Ellie was pregnant with twins.

Sally touched Tom's knee. "Are there more twins we don't know about?"

"Oh, yeah," Tom said. "My father was a twin, too. But his brother, my uncle Ransom, was lost at sea during World War II."

"That's so sad," Grace said, keeping an eagle eye on little Rosie and Lily as they dug in the sand with their colorful plastic shovels.

"Yeah." Tom sipped his beer. "My dad never accepted it though. He always had a feeling that his brother was still alive somewhere. You know, that twin radar of his wouldn't let him give up on his brother."

"So you could have an uncle living somewhere?" Sally said, her eyes wide. "Have you ever tried to find him?"

"No," Tom said, then started to laugh. "But something tells me I've just given you a new project to dig your teeth into."

"Yes, you have," Sally said with a big smile. "And I can't wait."

Aidan chuckled. If anyone could do it, Sally could. She had been a widow for many years and had spent part of that time trying to track down her late husband's brother, Tom, otherwise known as Aidan and Logan's dad. When Sally finally found him, the two had fallen in love, so who better than Sally to search for a lost uncle?

"You have to admit she's good at finding people," Logan said.

Aidan met Ellie's soft gaze and he felt the familiar jolt of happiness he always got when he looked at his beautiful wife. "She helped me find you."

"I think we found each other," Ellie whispered.

No thanks to his own stubbornness, Aidan thought silently as he gripped her hand in his. Thank goodness he'd come to his senses in time.

Now as he stretched his legs out on the chaise longue he shared with his wife, he considered himself the luckiest man on the planet. Ellie enriched his life in so many ways and he tried each day to show her how much love and happiness he held in his heart for her. They were perfect partners in every way possible and had given each other exactly what Ellie had always wanted and what Aidan had finally discovered he wanted just as badly. A family of their own.

* * * * *

COMING NEXT MONTH from Harlequin Desire®
AVAILABLE JUNE 4, 2013

#2233 SUNSET SEDUCTION
The Slades of Sunset Ranch
Charlene Sands
When the chance to jump into bed with longtime crush Lucas Slade comes along, Audrey Thomas can't help but seize it. Now the tricky part is to wrangle her way into the rich rancher's *heart*.

#2234 AFFAIRS OF STATE
Daughters of Power: The Capital
Jennifer Lewis
Can Ariella Winthrop—revealed as the secret love child of the U.S. president—find love with a royal prince whose family disapproves of her illegitimacy?

#2235 HIS FOR THE TAKING
Rich, Rugged Ranchers
Ann Major
It's been six years since Maddie Gray left town in disgrace. But now she's back, and wealthy rancher John Coleman can't stay away from the lover who once betrayed him.

#2236 TAMING THE LONE WOLFF
The Men of Wolff Mountain
Janice Maynard
Security expert Larkin Wolff lives by a code, but when he's hired to protect an innocent heiress, he's tempted to break all his rules and become *personally* involved with his client....

#2237 HOLLYWOOD HOUSE CALL
Jules Bennett
When an accident forces receptionist Callie Matthews to move in with her boss, her relationship with the sexy doctor becomes much less about business and *very* much about pleasure....

#2238 THE FIANCÉE CHARADE
The Pearl House
Fiona Brand
Faced with losing custody of her daughter, Gemma O'Neill will do anything—even pretend to be engaged to the man who fathered her child.

HDCNM0513

REQUEST YOUR FREE BOOKS!
2 FREE NOVELS PLUS 2 FREE GIFTS!

Ⓗ HARLEQUIN®

Desire

ALWAYS POWERFUL, PASSIONATE AND PROVOCATIVE

YES! Please send me 2 FREE Harlequin Desire® novels and my 2 FREE gifts (gifts are worth about $10). After receiving them, if I don't wish to receive any more books, I can return the shipping statement marked "cancel." If I don't cancel, I will receive 6 brand-new novels every month and be billed just $4.55 per book in the U.S. or $4.99 per book in Canada. That's a savings of at least 13% off the cover price! It's quite a bargain! Shipping and handling is just 50¢ per book in the U.S. and 75¢ per book in Canada.* I understand that accepting the 2 free books and gifts places me under no obligation to buy anything. I can always return a shipment and cancel at any time. Even if I never buy another book, the two free books and gifts are mine to keep forever.

225/326 HDN F4ZC

Name	(PLEASE PRINT)	
Address		Apt. #
City	State/Prov.	Zip/Postal Code

Signature (if under 18, a parent or guardian must sign)

Mail to the **Harlequin® Reader Service:**

IN U.S.A.: P.O. Box 1867, Buffalo, NY 14240-1867
IN CANADA: P.O. Box 609, Fort Erie, Ontario L2A 5X3

Want to try two free books from another line?
Call 1-800-873-8635 or visit www.ReaderService.com.

* Terms and prices subject to change without notice. Prices do not include applicable taxes. Sales tax applicable in N.Y. Canadian residents will be charged applicable taxes. Offer not valid in Quebec. This offer is limited to one order per household. Not valid for current subscribers to Harlequin Desire books. All orders subject to credit approval. Credit or debit balances in a customer's account(s) may be offset by any other outstanding balance owed by or to the customer. Please allow 4 to 6 weeks for delivery. Offer available while quantities last.

Your Privacy—The Harlequin® Reader Service is committed to protecting your privacy. Our Privacy Policy is available online at www.ReaderService.com or upon request from the Harlequin Reader Service.

We make a portion of our mailing list available to reputable third parties that offer products we believe may interest you. If you prefer that we not exchange your name with third parties, or if you wish to clarify or modify your communication preferences, please visit us at www.ReaderService.com/consumerchoice or write to us at Harlequin Reader Service Preference Service, P.O. Box 9062, Buffalo, NY 14269. Include your complete name and address.

HD13R

SPECIAL EXCERPT FROM

HARLEQUIN®

Desire

presents

SUNSET SEDUCTION

The latest installment of USA TODAY *bestselling author*

Charlene Sands's miniseries

THE SLADES OF SUNSET RANCH

All grown up, Audrey Faith Thomas seizes her chance to act on a teenage crush. Now she must face the consequences....

*U*sually not much unnerved Audrey Faith Thomas, except for the time when her big brother was bucked off Old Stormy at an Amarillo rodeo and broke his back.

Audrey shuddered at the memory and thanked the Almighty that Casey was alive and well and bossy as ever. But as she sat behind the wheel of her car, driving toward her fate, the fear coursing through her veins had nothing to do with her brother's disastrous five-second ride. This fear was much different. It made her want to turn her Chevy pickup truck around and go home to Reno and forget all about showing up at Sunset Ranch unannounced.

To face Lucas Slade.

The man she'd seduced and then abandoned in the middle of the night.

Audrey swallowed hard. She still couldn't believe what she'd done.

Last month, after an argument and a three week standoff with her brother, she'd ventured to his Lake Tahoe cabin to

HDEXPO513

make amends. He'd been right about the boyfriend she'd just dumped and she'd needed Casey's strong shoulder to cry on.

The last person she'd expected to find there was Luke Slade—the man she'd measured every other man against—sleeping in the guest room bed, *her bed*. Luke was the guy she'd crushed on during her teen years while traveling the rodeo circuit with Casey.

Seeing him had sent all rational thoughts flying out the window. This was her chance. She wouldn't let her prudish upbringing interfere with what she needed. When he rasped, "Come closer," in the darkened room, she'd taken that as an invitation to climb into bed with him, consequences be damned.

Well…she'd gotten a lot more than a shoulder to cry on, and it had been glorious.

Now she would finally come face-to-face with Luke. She'd confront him about the night they'd shared and confess her love for him, if it came down to that. She wondered what he thought about her abandoning him that night.

She would soon find out.

Find out what happens when Audrey and Luke reunite in

SUNSET SEDUCTION
by Charlene Sands.

Available June 2013 from Harlequin® Desire®
wherever books are sold!

HDEXPO513

HARLEQUIN®

A *Romance* FOR EVERY MOOD™

Stay up-to-date on all your romance-reading news with the *Harlequin Shopping Guide*, featuring bestselling authors, exciting new miniseries, books to watch and more!

The newest issue will be delivered right to you with our compliments! There are 4 each year.

Signing up is easy.

EMAIL

ShoppingGuide@Harlequin.ca

WRITE TO US

HARLEQUIN BOOKS
Attention: Customer Service Department
P.O. Box 9057, Buffalo, NY 14269-9057

OR PHONE

1-800-873-8635 in the United States
1-888-343-9777 in Canada

Please allow 4-6 weeks for delivery of the first issue by mail.

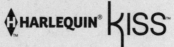